# My Heart Will Go On And On

*Love Stories*

Dr. Harmeet Kaur Bhalla

First published in 2021 by
Becomeshakespeare.com

One Point Six Technologies Pvt Ltd.119-123, 1st Floor, Building J2, B - Wing, WadalaTruck Terminal, Wadala East, Mumbai, Maharashtra, India, 400022.T:+91 8080226699



© ISBN - 978-93-5458-243-1

# Preface

The four-letter word 'LOVE' has varied interpretations. It began with Adam and Eve and has thereafter spread its branches all around this vast universe. Love is a sensual feeling to be experienced. It cannot be defined in a second or a minute; it takes ages to grasp its true essence. It is a feeling that arises from the subconscious mind and then travels to the heart. It can happen anytime, anywhere and at any age.

Compatibility in love is the biggest factor that leads to its success. It leads to love between two people who unite to get married. They give a legal name to their relationship. Marriage is an institution that brings together two separate individuals irrespective of their caste, creed, and culture. Infidelity leads to failure in intimacy.

This collection of ten short stories brings out the true fragrance of love in its many forms. It makes you cry as well as laugh. It makes you enter a world where life becomes meaningful.

It is believed that marriages are made in heaven. Sometimes you know the other person for ages while at times he or she is a stranger. Life is incomplete if we are devoid of a partner. If love is deliberately forced, the result often proves to be disastrous. Some are head over heels in love with each other and they are ready to face the challenges that come along with that level of emotions. We have to comprehend the fact that love heals the world and is unbeatable.

# Contents

# *The Flute of Krishna*

In the village of Kapilavastu, the temples were being demolished. The Mughals were plundering as well as looting gold and precious jewels from the temples. King Sayyed Ali of Faisalabad wanted to expand the Mughal Empire so he started targeting the Hindus and their temples. On the outskirts of the city was a small temple named 'Devkinandan'. The temple had silver statues of Krishna and Radha. The priest Sudarshan took care of the temple. He slept in a tiny room situated behind the temple.

They were five hundred in all when they attacked this small temple. Sudarshan, being alone, was almost dead in the attack. The most precious things present in the temple were the diamond-studded flute and the silver idols. King Sayyed Ali and his men had an eye on them. They attacked the temple, broke the walls and carried away the idols of Krishna and Radha. From the corner of his eye, Sudarshan watched the dazzling flute being pulled mercilessly and taken away. He lay wounded with tears rolling down his eyes.

After this, the King moved towards the city. The second most beloved thing of Kapilavastu was Annapurna. An ardent devotee of Lord Krishna, her beauty was known in all the cities situated near Kapilavastu. With fair complexion, black eyes and full lips she was the cynosure of every bachelor's eyes of the state. Annapurna was the only daughter of a poor farmer and he deeply loved his daughter. Sayyed Ali came to this city with a dual purpose. He wanted the precious flute and Annapurna.

"You will be my third queen," said Sayyed Ali to Annapurna whose father Premchand held his feet and lay on the ground begging him to leave his daughter and him alone.

"Help me," urged Annapurna to her father and hugged him tightly. She did not want to waste the fruitful years of her life with the Mughals. But, to no avail.

With a heavy heart, Annapurna left her parents. She was made to sit on the beautifully decorated elephant and carried away by the enemy. Sayyed Ali left with his troops to Faisalabad. He was a ruler famous for his callous behaviour. He despised the Hindus and wanted to rule the country, so he kept attacking temples all over India.

Annapurna was given a grand welcome at the palace. She was given a large room with several maids at her service. She found these things quite uncomfortable. She was made to learn the royal lifestyle by her two senior maids Shahin and Ruksana. Every morning they dressed her up and took her to the Royal Hall of the king. The women of Faisalabad were envious of her beauty.

One day Queen Annapurna went for a walk in the palace garden with King Sayyed Ali. He deeply loved his queen and placed her above all. The queen was away from her Lord Krishna. She was already missing her morning prayers and her visit to the temple. "Can I go to the temple to pray, my lord?" she asked the king almost stammering. "How dare you ask such a question in my territory," shrieked the king. "I am destroying temples and you want to visit one…never ask such a question." The queen was unaware of his motives and her heart ached at the mere thought of the temples being destroyed and her Lord being turned to ruins.

Early one morning she ran out on hearing some commotion outside her room. She was shocked to see Sayyed Ali lying on the ground. The guards picked him up and made him lay down on the bed in his room. The local Vaidya was summoned urgently. He patted Sayyed Ali's face and in a few minutes, he gained consciousness. The Vaidya examined him thoroughly.

"Maharani, the king is suffering from high fever and he needs rest. I am giving the required medicines. Don't let him go out until he recovers," said the Vaidya. The queen sat by her husband's bedside and pressed his forehead. The King loved Annapurna and was greatly concerned for her. Days passed into weeks; the condition of the King started deteriorating day by day. There were no signs of improvement.

One night, the king had a strange dream. In the dream, he saw himself being led to a dense jungle by a shadow. He reached the gates of a temple and the shadow threw him at the steps. He started moaning with acute pain when suddenly someone splashed water at his face. He woke up with a jerk, "Where am I…. save me…. please don't throw me." He saw himself surrounded by a dozen of people, his three wives and the Vaidya. The King rubbed his eyes and shouted, "Get lost all of you…leave me alone…. I am alright…go away." All of them left the room but the queens stayed. They made him sit and gave him water and syrups to drink. The King narrated his dream to his Queens and told them, "It seems I have very little time left now and I am not keeping well. I would like to hand over all valuables and kingdom to the three of you and our children. Annapurna, you are so young and innocent. You are dearest and the one closest to my heart. You have no children and I am afraid the enemy will kidnap you in my absence as they have an eye on you."

Annapurna started crying and sat on the bedside holding his feet, "My Lord, I cannot live without you…. I am your obedient wife. Where will I go?"

He spoke feebly, "Tell the soldiers to open the vault and carry the valuables to my room. Tell the children to come in the evening. Annapurna you sit with me." The two queens left. Annapurna came and started pressing his forehead. He held her hand and said, "I have loved you since the day I first saw you but now I am worried…. I have demolished and ransacked temples…I didn't even allow you to pray to your Lord Krishna. I am worried about your future; you can go back and live your life."

"No, my lord…. I have no one except you…you will soon be well."

After half an hour the soldiers started bringing the trunks carrying precious jewels, gold statues, diamond-studded swords and many other expensive things. Half of the king's room began glistening with the items he had robbed. The King held Annapurna's hand and started crying," Oh God…. I have sinned….be merciful…. riches don't attract me anymore."

The two queens entered with their six sons - the eldest Altaf, twenty and the youngest Murad, five. Both the queens had three sons each. The king ordered his sons to divide the items equally into three parts.

"Annapurna, you will get the third share…. you can take and live in any one of my three palaces," said the king pitifully looking at her.

Annapurna got up from the bed and moved towards the valuables. Her eyes were searching for something. She came up to the king and said, "My Lord…. I don't want my share…. I want only one thing…. the flute of Krishna which you brought from the temple in my hometown."

Altaf was busy separating the tangled necklaces when he got a glimpse of the jewel-studded flute lying in one corner of the trunk. He called her, "Mother, it is here." Annapurna walked fast and caught hold of it. She held it close to her heart as the King watched her from his bed. He thought he had done injustice to her, and her faith in her Lord will help her sail smoothly in the ship of life. He called her in a soft voice, "Annapurna…. keep this flute under my pillow…it is very dear to me…. come here…you can pray in my palace too…. let them take their share to their rooms." She gently placed the flute under his pillow. He soon became unconscious again and the Vaidya was summoned. After examining his pulse, he said, "The King is suffering from a strange fever and showing no chances of recovery…. he will gain consciousness when his fever subsides." The Queens were equally concerned but Annapurna was the worst affected.

The King remained stable for two days. On the third day he

opened his eyes. The third queen wiped his forehead and smiled. He said, "Where am I….my body is aching….am I still alive…. help me Allah…be merciful."

"No, my lord…. see your kingdom…. you have to take care of your people…. you will get well soon," said Annapurna sobbing incessantly. The King couldn't speak properly. He picked up his hand slowly and signalled Annapurna to come closer to him. Then, he said, "I don't know why I am still living…there must be a reason…. I have one last wish."

"Yes, my Lord…. we will fulfil it," said Annapurna

"I feel I have done injustice to you and your lord…. oh……ahh," said Sayyed Ali and went on coughing. In the meantime, the Vaidya came inside and gave him some syrup to drink. The King continued, "Annapurna my dearest queen…. I want you to take me to Kapilavastu so that I can apologize to God…. take me."

"My Lord, you are not in the position….it will take more than fifteen days to reach there and you cannot travel for so many days."

"I want ……please take me…. before dying…Oh God, grant me my last wish….my love for you will be complete…. the day I take you back and hand you over to him…. I will die peacefully…. I will be at ease…. that there is someone to take care of you."

The arrangements were done and the Vaidya's, servants, soldiers ,Annapurna with horses and elephants started their journey to Kapilavastu. The King was made to lie down on a special bed which was carried by four of his servants. The queen took care of him in the entire journey and something was keeping him alive. At night, the tent houses were set and they took rest. The king became weak and wanted to reach Kapilavastu as quickly as possible.

After eighteen days they reached the city of Kapilavastu. The king opened his eyes and told his wife to take him to the temple. She too was tired and ordered the soldiers, "Turn towards the road that leads to the temple….be slow…the road is uneven." The convoy moved forward with the King lying on the wooden bed. He looked at Annapurna with his agonizing eyes and smiled as the destination was near. They covered the rough path and reached there in an hour.

On hearing thousands of footsteps, the people started running and hiding indoors. The Mughals already held a bad reputation. Their movement on the temple road was not palatable for the people of Kapilavastu. The temple was already in a dilapidated condition and the people were greatly confused. They didn't want any more destruction in their town.

The King and Queen reached the temple. Tears of happiness flowed down their cheeks. The temple walls were broken and two stone sculptures were placed on a wooden plank. It was then covered with a white cloth tied on the four sides to trees.

Sudarshan rushed to greet them and fell at their feet, pleading he said with his hands folded, "My Lord…. have mercy on us….my Lord, please don't do any harm now…. let it remain as it is…we are not building any temple…. Annapurna didi…. save us…save your Lord…. save Krishna and Radha."

The King instructed his soldiers to put down his bed. He told them to make him stand straight. With their help, he got down from the bed and told them to carry him to the temple. In these three weeks, the King had started looking very gaunt and worn out. He called Annapurna and said, "Tell my men to bring down the trunk kept on the elephant…. bring it…get it down."

His men got down the trunk and brought it to the king. He handed them a key from his pocket and told them to unlock it. Annapurna went close to the king. He held her hand and said, "You have given me solace and I want you to open this trunk." As Annapurna bent down and opened the trunk, she was astonished to see what was inside. With trembling hands, she turned towards the king and said, "My Lord, God will be merciful to you…. you have done your duty."

"Bend down …. take them out," said the king to his queen. She took out the idols from the trunk one by one and then finally took out the jewel-studded flute. The king signalled her to hand him the flute and moved towards the temple. With slow steps, he crossed the broken walls with Sudarshan following him. He sat near the stone idols and with weak, delicate hands picked them up and gave them to Sudarshan. He instructed Annapurna to hand him the silver idols. He placed them on the wooden plank and brought the flute forward.

The people of the town were gazing at all these happenings. They had tears and smiles on their faces. The king placed the flute on the Lord's idol and folded his hands. Annapurna was left speechless and she kept holding him. Suddenly she felt as if his hands were slithering away gradually. She shrieked and called the Vaidya and he rushed to see the king. He patted the king's cheeks and picked up his hand to feel the pulse, "I am sorry…. your majesty…. the queen… I am sorry. He has done his duty and fulfilled his promise to God…there are no boundaries in love."

The queen closed his eyes with her warm hands and said, "You took me away from my Lord but …. today you have brought me back….and gifted me to my Lord…. from today onwards this is my…. palace….my home….my temple of love."

# *1984*

It was the 31st of October, eleven in the morning. Ajooni stood at her window watching people running helter-skelter. Her husband Yuvraj had left for his work as usual at nine and she had slowly started completing her daily chores. That day she didn't switch on the radio as she was unwell. In her ninth month of pregnancy, she knew she would have to go to the hospital the moment her labour pains started. Her mother- in-law Sukhjot Kaur was a religious lady. She went up to Ajooni who was still standing and asked her, "I hope you are well…. go and sit or take rest…. just switch on the television…. let me see is there something special. Why are these people shouting? Let me close the door." She quickly went up to the door and bolted it. Ajooni switched on the television and was horror-struck on hearing the news "Beeji! Come here, watch the news…What is going around the country…. What will happen now.Should I call Yuvraj?!" she yelled.

"Yes, my child he must have reached the shop…. just tell him to come back," said Sukhjot gravely rubbing her hands. Ajooni dialled the office number but did not get any response. "I hope he reaches in time…. should I call Balraj…. he is still sleeping."

Sukhjot had two sons; the elder Yuvraj, who had just celebrated his first marriage anniversary a week ago and the younger, Balraj a twenty-one-year-old lad who was pursuing his post-graduation from a local college in their city of Mirzapur. Sukhjot had lost her husband when her children were aged five and three. She had taught in a school and brought up her children. Yuvraj began his own electronics business with little investment in the main Sadar Bazaar. He married his high school love Ajooni and Sukhjot never opposed this marriage. Ajooni was more of a daughter than a daughter-in-law.

Sukhjot reached Balraj's room and shook him up, "Wake up…. see what is happening everywhere…. dress up quickly." He jumped out of the bed and stood straight and started tying his hair. "Beeji…. why are you so upset…I will see to everything," he said patting his mother's cheeks, and walked towards the washroom.

Within five minutes there was a loud knock at the door. Sukhjot peeped out through the window and saw their neighbour, Mrs Shaista Khan, at the door. She was a fair-complexioned, middle-aged lady with a lovely smile. She had covered her face and only her large hazel eyes were visible.

She almost whispered on seeing her, "Open the door…Sukh Didi… open the door."

Sukhjot rushed towards the door and opened it to see a few people standing outside her gate. Shaista came in breathing heavily and closed the door tightly. She went up to Ajooni, caught hold of her hand and said, "I hope you are well…. where are Yuvraj and Balraj…. let them stay indoors."

"Aunty…. Why have these people gathered outside?" asked Ajooni.

"Riots have begun all over the country after the assassination. Sikhs are being searched for and killed. The people outside were enquiring about your house but somehow, I managed to make my way……. Stay indoors…. if any emergency arises you can call me…. you have my phone number….my backdoor will be open." Saying this, she peeped out and continued, "I am worried …. hope everything goes on well."

In the meantime, Ajooni kept dialling Yuvraj's number but it was constantly going unanswered. The crowd started shouting on top of their voice, "Kill the sinners…kill the murderers." Sukhjot caught hold of Ajooni and said, "Keep calling him". Then, she folded her hands and said, "Waheguru keep my son safe." Ajooni sat down on the chair near the phone.

Balraj entered dressed in his white shirt, blue jeans and black turban. He was about to open the door when his mother came up to him and held his hand, "Don't open the door ....so many people are standing outside.... I don't know what they are up to." She started sobbing, "Yuvraj is not picking up the phone."

In the meantime, the crowd started banging the gate and Shaista caught hold of their hand and pulled them towards the back door. Balraj became adamant and said, "You take them, aunty.... I will take care of the house.... I will see them."

"No…....no… my son they are multiplying and we are helpless…. come with us," shouted his mother. Balraj a young, energetic boy found difficulty in comprehending the reason for these sudden behavioural changes in the people. The news on the television declared the death of the leader and it seemed as if they would break their gate and come inside. Shaista moved with the three towards the backdoor. They had no time to look at their belongings. Sukhjot wanted to pick up her jewellery. She rushed to open the almirah and grabbed everything that was kept in front. She kept her valuables in the black purse and walked fast. They didn't have enough time. Ajooni walked carefully with the bag she had prepared for the hospital.

As soon as they entered Shaista's house from her backdoor, they heard rioters entering their house. The three of them heard loud voices, "Search for them…. they ran away…. go to the terrace…. kill them." The hooligans were throwing their valuables and looting their household items. They sat in one room locked from outside, crying over the strange happenings but were thankful to Shaista. In the meantime, Ajooni started feeling uneasy and Sukhjot could make out from her expressions that she will have to be taken to the hospital anyhow. She made her lie down and called Shaista from the window. She unlocked the door and entered with tea and biscuits.

Sukhjot spoke with tears running down on her cheeks, "Shaista… you are our saviour…thank you". She embraced her and she continued,

"I think Ajooni has to be taken to the hospital…. she is having labour pains.How will we manage?" Balraj watched his sister-in-law and was equally concerned. He said sitting with both his hands on his forehead, "Aunty, you people have locked me inside…I need to go out and throw these rascals out." He started running out but they caught hold of him. Sukhjot pushed him down on the bed and screamed, "Go…. give yourself to them…. I too will come with you…. leave Ajooni…. let her suffer… come." She started howling and Shaista came and caught hold of her. Ajooni started sobbing and came up to Sukhjot and folded her hands, "Mamma…please…. stay indoors…. Balraj I have no information about Yuvraj…Waheguru keep him safe…. Aunty you will have to arrange a doctor…. probably an ambulance…. I can't wait anymore." Shaista rushed to her husband Faizal who was sitting at his main door so that and whispered, "We need to arrange an ambulance…. Ajooni is having labour pains."

They contacted the hospital and called up the nearest police station. They preferred to wait for another hour; by then, the crowd had moved further. The ambulance came with the police jeep and halted outside the Khan Bungalow. Mr Faizal Khan creeped out and opened the gate. Two men and a nurse came inside with a stretcher. Shaista handed her a bag full of clothes for them and Balraj handed her some money. Sukhjot gave a tight hug to Balraj and said, "You promise me that you will not go out…. keep enquiring about your brother…take care." She sat in the ambulance with Ajooni on the stretcher. Suddenly her eyes moved towards her house and she almost shrieked on seeing the doors open with all the household items lying scattered everywhere. They had looted their house. She looked at the pale-faced Ajooni and preferred to stay mute. The entire city was burning and Sikhs were being thrown into the fire. She remembered Yuvraj and kept looking outside as if her eyes were searching for him.

They reached the hospital in half an hour. Ajooni's condition was becoming critical. The doctors on duty took her straight to the labour room. Sukhjot sat on the bench outside lost in thoughts, weary and depressed. Her eyes were swollen and blank and the memories of her dilapidated house with scattered belongings sent shivers down the spine. Everything present in the house were bought one by one with the money she had earned by burning the candles at both ends. She thought of Yuvraj and started chanting her prayers. She wanted him to be with his wife at this most awaited moment of their life.

"It's a boy," said the Doctor to Sukhjot lost in thoughts. She shuddered and stood up saying, "Thank you, doctor… are the mother and child well?"

"Yes Madam…. they are fine,"

"Can I see them?" said Sukhjot with tears of happiness flowing down her eyes.

"In an hour she will be shifted to the room."

For a week, Sukhjot looked after the infant and Ajooni day and night. Every single day she called up Balraj once and enquired about Yuvraj. Her tension kept building as she had to think of a genuine answer for Ajooni every day regarding her son. She too was equally worried. The news channels and newspapers were displaying the day-to-day disastrous happenings. There was no way out so she preferred to stay in the hospital for a few more days.

One morning Shaista heard an ambulance and a police siren outside Sukhjot's house. She locked Balraj's room and rushed out with Faizal. One of them opened the backdoor and got down from the ambulance. He looked at the house number and the other one came up to Faizal and said, "Does this house belong to Yuvraj Singh?"

"Yes…...yes…what is the matter…. tell me," cried Shaista and caught hold of Faizal's arm.

The driver got down and said, "Is there no one in the house? We have brought the dead body of Yuvraj Singh. It was lying in his shop…... burnt…. but the address was known by the other shopkeepers….is there anybody to take the dead body?"

Shaista screamed and ran up to the ambulance and Faizal followed her. In the ambulance lay Yuvraj, charred from head to foot with his hair lying open. She climbed up and caught hold of his feet. She said, "Wake up…. you have become a dad…your mom is still waiting for you." Faizal told them about Sukhjot and Ajooni. They made her get down; she opened the doors of her house and they carried his dead body to their house. They handed over the dead body to them officially and left. In the meantime, the neighbours gathered and Shaista ran inside to tell Balraj. He came out and fell on Yuvraj's body and started patting his face, "Come back, brother…. you didn't even see your son…. how will I tell them?"

The cremation was held; Balraj didn't inform his mother and Ajooni. He extended their stay in the hospital. After fifteen days, things started returning to normal again and Balraj gathered courage and went to his house. He had to begin from scratch; he knew it would take years. He was their only support. He settled his house with the help of his neighbours and decided to call them back from the hospital.

Sukhjot, Ajooni and baby Yuvraj entered the house and Shaista made them sit on a chair. She took the baby in her arms. Balraj was the one who broke the news of Yuvraj and there was shouting and screaming. Both of them fainted on the spot. The neighbours proved to be helpful in this hour of distress. Balraj looked at them with wide-open blank eyes.

A year passed. Balraj left his studies so that he could look after the shop. Financially they suffered but Sukhjot managed to pull them out of the swamp. She took out all her savings from the bank and handed them to Balraj. Ajooni started looking pale and gloomy. She hardly conversed with them and passed most of her time with baby Yuvraj. The boy was named Yuvraj because they wanted him to be alive forever in their hearts. Sukhjot's heart ached on seeing the innocent and lovely Ajooni lost in thoughts. She couldn't spoil her life. She was more of a daughter and she had to be married again but with whom? She didn't want to send Yuvraj away. She was in a dilemma. She had to go for the final decision to Balraj.

When Balraj came home that night from the shop he started playing with Yuvraj. He then went to the living room and Sukhjyot served him dinner. After dinner, he went to his room to do his daily accounts. He had taken over the business and after months of hard labour, it had started running smoothly.

Sukhjot came over to his room and sat down on the chair next to him, "Balraj did you have a look at Ajooni lately…. she is sinking day by day…. we have to see to her future…. she has always looked up to us in hours of trouble."

"What do you want to do for her…. we are taking good care of her…. rest, you can ask her…we can think something about her future life," replied Balraj engrossed in his accounts. He continued, "Even I have something to tell."

"What is it about? You have to tell me first," asked Sukhjot with curiosity arising every second and she caught hold of his hand. Balraj looked up to her, kept his pen down and said, "Even I wanted to discuss my love life…..... I'm in love with Sohni….my high school classmate…. once you find a suitable groom for Ajooni, I can get married after that."

Sukhjot felt her hands and feet going numb. She tried to gather strength and continued with tears streaming down her eyes, "Balraj, you are my only son now and Yuvraj is with us in the form of his son, I can see the same eyes, hair and habits in him…. he is still with us…. I can't stay away from him."

Balraj caught hold of her and wiped her tears with his hand and said, "How can we manage like this …. she has to leave the house if she gets married…. you have to make up your mind…the doors of this house are always open for her."

"But Balraj…. if you get married to the girl of your choice…. I know nothing about her and all of a sudden…. I am worried about

Ajooni's future."

"Ma…. please…leave your emotions aside…. Please," said Balraj folding his hands in front of her. Sukhjot started sobbing and became uncontrollable and she said, "Balraj have you made a promise to that girl? You should have discussed it with me."

"How could I…. Yuvraj's death had left us shattered…now I thought is the appropriate time…... I too can settle down," said he placing both his hands on her shoulder.

"Balraj, you will have to give it a second thought…. I want you to marry Ajooni and give your name to her child," said Sukhjot in a little strict tone. Balraj put down his hands and sat on the chair looking at his mother blank-faced.

"What!? How could you even think like this…...? I have always respected Ajooni and equally loved her child…. but I can never dream of such a relationship…. leave me alone." Sukhjot found his face getting red with anger but she had to speak up and make him realise that he too held the responsibility of this family now. She came out of the room and felt as if she had done her duty; rest lay in the hands of Waheguru.

The next morning, Sukhjot went up to Balraj's room with a cup of tea and drew the curtains so that the sunshine could enter his room. She waited for a ray of hope. She woke him up and handed him his bed tea. His eyes were swollen as if he had cried. She sat on the corner of the bed near his feet and said, "My son…I love you and I am your well-wisher."

Balraj rubbed his eyes and told her, "You better call Ajooni……. I want to make it clear with her. Have you told her?"

"Not yet…. I wanted to ask you first."

"Call her…. Ajooni…Ajooni…. where is she," he said in an authoritative tone.

Ajooni entered breathing heavily with baby Yuvraj in her arms and asked, "What happened? Balraj…...ma…. is everything okay?"

Sukhjot ordered her to sit down and said, "Ajooni…I am worried about your future…. I want to ask you about getting settled in life again…you can't live a barren and cold life…. meaningless…. you need a life partner."

Ajooni's throat was choked and she was speechless. Words came out with great difficulty and with a heavy voice, she said, "Ma, you know I have loved only one man in my life…. Yuvraj…. only Yuvraj…I cannot even think of someone else…he was my life…he has given me a new life…I'm sorry." She hugged her baby tightly with tears flowing continuously.

Sukhjot came up to wipe her tears and she too couldn't control herself, "But…. I want you to settle down…. I want you to marry Balraj." Ajooni stood up suddenly with a jerk. She wiped her face with her stole and gravely said, "Ma, how could you even think of it…. I have always seen him as my younger brother…. please…. please." She fell at her feet and continued, "Ma, let me live with his memories…I can't do injustice to him….and not even to Balraj…. not to Sohni." Sukhjot stood stupefied on hearing her name and looked at Balraj. She then turned again towards Ajooni and asked, "Do you know her?"

"Yes, I know her very well…. she is a decent girl…. you couldn't have got a better girl than Sohni…she's the best match for Balraj… Ma…. let them live happily," said Ajooni settling her stole and dismantled hair. She looked so pretty and innocent. Sukhjot's dreams were not shattered but were given a different angle and she decided to go with their decision. A decision that would be healthy for their family.

A week passed and Sohni's parents turned up to meet their family. The wedding was fixed after two weeks. It would be a simple wedding because the scars of the horrendous happenings had not yet healed. They were still fresh and scary. The wedding took place in a nearby

Gurudwara. The bride looking stunning in red and the bridegroom, alluring in a grey suit. There were very few people invited and by five in the evening they reached home. Sukhjot and Ajooni welcomed Sohni to her new house.

The next morning all of them sat at the breakfast table and Ajooni tried to explain to Sohni several things related to their family. After having breakfast, she said, "Sohni, you are welcome to this small family of ours. You were a part of our family earlier too and already know the traumas we have gone through." She took out a letter from her pocket and handed it to Balraj. He opened it and started reading. After reading he looked up towards Ajooni and asked, "What is this? Where are you planning to go?"

Sukhjot got tensed and asked him, "What is written in this letter?"

Balraj handed it to Sukhjot and looked towards Ajooni, "When did you plan all this? You didn't even inform us. How will you manage? We are there for you…. Yuvraj and you are our responsibility."

Sukhjot got up from the chair and came up to Ajooni and softly placed her hands on her shoulder and said, "This is your joining letter from St. Thomas Girl's School Nainital…you are joining there as a hostel warden…...you didn't even tell me…. you can't leave us."

Ajooni got up from the chair and embraced Sukhjot and said, "Ma, you are not alone now…Sohni is there to take care of everyone…. just wait for a second." After saying this she went to Yuvraj's room and carried him in her arms. He was fast asleep. With tears streaming down her eyes she took him and handed him to Sohni. "You are his mother from today….in happiness and sorrow….in highs and lows…. he will look up to you for everything." She turned to Sukhjot and said, "Your son will always stay with you…...he will never leave you…. but I need to live one more life…. with his memories…. he was my only love."

Sukhjot had tears in her eyes. She begged Ajooni to stay back but she had made up her mind. She had to leave the next morning, so till midnight all of them helped her in packing her bags. The next morning all of them went to the railway station and Balraj helped her in boarding the train. Sohni embraced her while he touched her feet and said, "Ajooni…you have the right to live life according to your choice…. but whenever you feel low or tired, you are welcome back…. this house belongs to you……and we have taken one more decision…. Yuvraj will be our only child…his love will never be shared." Ajooni got on the train and sat in her seat. She had loved, lost and sacrificed, maybe that was written in her destiny. The train started leaving the platform slowly.

# The Cherry Blossoms

It was six in the evening - almost dark - when Cynthia hastened her steps to take shelter under the thick elm tree as it had started raining cats and dogs. There was seldom rain in October at Darjeeling; but today was one of those rare days. The couple standing next to her was also getting wet. The man looked pale and sick; he held a thick black walking stick, and was finding it difficult to stand. Cynthia couldn't keep to herself, and thus she started enquiring about his health.

"Aunty, is Uncle unwell?" she asked gently. The old lady replied patiently, "We had come to visit the doctor, but suddenly the weather has turned unpleasant."

From the corner of her eyes, the old lady watched Cynthia. For two years Mrs. Williams had come across several girls with diverse backgrounds for her only son Eshan. Mrs and Mr Williams knew that a well-qualified, affluent girl would never adjust. She will have to set certain boundaries. Cynthia's innocence and generosity spoke in itself. Mrs Williams finally asked her, "What is your name, child?

Cynthia hesitatingly answered, "I'm Cynthia. I live in the 'Blessings' orphanage at the corner of the Mall Road."

The lady replied generously, "We are Mrs and Mr Williams and we live next to the Sunrise Bakery." The rain slowed down and the couple started walking down the lane. The road had become slippery due to the rain. Cynthia asked if she could help them out in reaching their destination, to which they readily agreed.

Mrs Williams was intrigued by this unknown female. The image of her eccentric, not-so-jovial son Eshan kept troubling her mind. He worked as a clerk in a private bank and sincerely loved his parents.

He mastered perfection but was callous and grew violent at times. He suffered from bipolar disorder but that remained a hidden factor.

October month was slightly cold. Cynthia accompanied Mrs and Mr Williams downhill to Dr Sanjay Verma's clinic. She left them outside the clinic.

It was 7.30 P.M and Mrs Brown was sitting on her armchair on the porch waiting for Cynthia. She enquired, "Why are you so late?" The children at the orphanage were hungry. Mrs. Brown was a childless widow. For twenty-five years she was running this orphanage. She owned this huge bungalow and several people lent a helping hand to her. Without delay, Cynthia entered the kitchen and quickly prepared dinner. There were fifteen children in all, aged five to twenty-five. Cynthia was the eldest and most charming. Deep blue eyes, sharp features, fair complexion, and her sublimity made her an apple of everyone's eye.

It took almost a week for Mrs and Mr Williams to convince Eshan and finally one Sunday morning he came up to his mother and said in a dominating tone, "I have some spare time today, so I can manage to go with you." Mrs William's happiness knew no bounds; she knew it was the will of God. It was quite relaxing for Mrs Williams that Eshan did not raise any objection to Cynthia being an orphan. She was yet to gather the exact information about Cynthia. At noon, they reached 'Blessings'. Mrs Brown welcomed them and the three-hour conversation seemed exhausting. Eshan couldn't refuse after having the very first look at Cynthia.

Mrs Brown had a special place in her heart for Cynthia and she wanted her to get married so that she could have a secure future. The Williams family held great respect in the Christian community of Darjeeling but she wanted Cynthia's approval. Cynthia was twenty-five years old now. After completing her Intermediate, she had done her three years diploma in nursing.

A strange feeling engulfed Cynthia from the moment she saw

Eshan. His curious looks and strange body movements gave her an uneasy feeling. In the evening Mrs Brown made Cynthia sit next to her and asked her, "Cynthia, my child, there's no rose without a thorn. See, you are mature enough to comprehend life. I would like to tell you that you have to enter this new life and Eshan seems to be a suitable match."

Parentless people have fewer options in life. Cynthia was one of them. She had spent sleepless nights questioning God about her faults and her identity in this drab world. That night she was questioning God again.

The next morning Mrs Brown called up Mrs Williams and cheerfully told her about Cynthia's consent for marriage. The marriage was fixed for the first week of December.

It was the 5th of December; the chilly winter had set in and the streets were crowded as it was the month widely chosen by the tourists. Very few close guests were invited to the wedding as Mrs Williams didn't want to give it air.

The bride and the groom arrived. Cynthia was the centre of attraction. She looked mesmerizing in minimal makeup and jewellery. Her inexpensive white gown and silver footwear did not diminish her beauty in the least. Eshan looked handsome in a white suit and a pink shirt. His tanned skin, dreamy eyes, and lithesome figure made him stand out from the rest.

The priest arrived; the guests were made to sit inside the Church. Vows and rings were exchanged and they finally became a couple. After lunch, gradually all the guests left. Tears of happiness rolled down Mrs Williams' eyes and she hugged Mrs Brown tightly. Cynthia and Eshan were made to sit in the car with Mrs Williams in the backseat and Mr. Williams sat in the front seat.

She was about to enter a place she could call her own with the people she would adore lifelong. A nameless, desolate girl of twenty-five imagines her man to be loaded with warmth and opulence.

A simple house with a small garden full of beautiful flowers seemed so welcoming. The house had wooden floors and antique furniture. Her favourite trees, the Cherry Blossoms, were missing.

The male world was an unfamiliar one for Cynthia. That night when she reached her room, Eshan hesitatingly came up and sat next to her. He didn't want his near and dear ones to take advantage so he disclosed all the dark secrets with which she had to stick lifelong. He told her about the bipolar disorder he was suffering from for seven years. He married her because he needed somebody to nurture him as his parents had grown old.

Cynthia's hands and feet went numb; her premonition had been right. The very first person that came into her mind was Mrs Brown. Was she aware of Eshan's illness or had she deliberately thrown her into this deep well? It was the beginning of an unprecedented life. That night, she questioned God again.

The next morning, she came out of her room with eyes swollen, hair tangled, and sat in the drawing-room. Mrs Williams greeted her and could easily make out the beginning of Cynthia's stressful life. She sat next to her and said in a tone full of guilt, "Maybe God punishes me for this sin but Eshan has many good qualities which you will come across gradually." Since that day Mrs Williams became her bosom friend.

After a few days, Christmas arrived. The hills looked resplendent at night. The city was lit up with exquisite lights and mistletoes bloomed all across the slopes. The hills echoed with Christmas carols and hymns. Since childhood, Cynthia had a special adoration for Cherry Blossoms. While driving down from Church that Christmas, she apprehensively told Eshan about her desire to plant pink Cherry Blossoms in their garden. On the way, they stopped at the nursery to buy two saplings. On reaching home they planted them on both sides of the main gate.

Two years passed and Cynthia was still trying to comprehend his behavioural patterns. He had to be regular with his medicines. At times he would have mood swings……either he would be extremely happy or there would be bouts of depression. Every day was a new day with some bizarre happenings in store for her. Mrs Williams thanked Cynthia every day for all the adjustments she was doing for Eshan's sake.

Love and relationship were a matter of choice for Eshan. But one thing which was quite gratifying for Mrs Williams was that Cynthia had accepted her son with all his pros and cons. At times he wouldn't speak to her for days and sometimes he wanted her day and night. Cynthia had developed an unconditional love for this man.

After two years of marriage one fine day, Cynthia broke the news to Mrs Williams that she had conceived. Dr Sanjay Verma's wife was a gynaecologist. Cynthia started going for her regular check-ups.

In March early one Sunday morning, Cynthia was taking a leisurely walk in the garden and watching her Cherry Blossoms grow. Suddenly a huge truck and a car came and took a halt outside the neighbouring house. A young handsome man got down the car and opened the gate. He had an unkempt look, protruding black eyes, Chevron moustache, fair complexion, and medium height.

That very afternoon due to the ear-splitting sounds from the neighbourhood Eshan started having his emotional highs. Cynthia quickly brought the medicine and made him gulp it down with water.

The next morning there was a slight knock at the door. Mr Williams walked slowly towards the door holding his stick and slowly opened the main door.

Seeing a new face, Mr. Williams asked inquisitively, "How can I help you?"

"I'm Nathan, your new neighbour," he replied. "I've just shifted from Shillong with my mother. She is unwell and I wanted to ask if there is a Doctor nearby," Nathan told worriedly.

Mr. Williams called Cynthia as only she could provide the required information. Cynthia came out of her room. She looked captivating in a pink gown. She was surprised to see the same man due to whom Eshan was unwell the previous day. She told him about the Doctor and enquired about this new stranger.

Nathan left the house thanking them. As soon as Cynthia stood up, she noticed Eshan standing near the bedroom door and watching her resentfully. A new behavioural pattern was developing. His immense love and possessiveness for Cynthia were noticeable. That night she questioned God again.

Every evening when Eshan returned from his office, he stood near the gate and stared at Nathan's house suspiciously. Something was disturbing his mind. On the other hand, Nathan started coming frequently to their place. The place was new for him so whenever he was in trouble, he dropped in.

In these few days, Cynthia noticed drastic changes in Eshan. He had started hitting her at times. If Mrs and Mr Williams had not been there to intervene, her condition would have become miserable.

Cynthia's seventh month had started and she found great difficulty in walking. The man whose child she was about to give birth to, seemed to her a stranger at times. The coming days became unbearable for Cynthia and her health started deteriorating.

Due to depression, Eshan's suspicion was growing day by day. It was creeping like a worm in his brain. The next evening when he returned from the office, he saw Nathan sitting in his drawing room with his parents. He didn't utter a word and walked straight to his room. That night after dinner, he went straight to his bedroom. He caught hold of Cynthia by her hair and started hitting her with his fist. He shrieked, "You bitch, don't try to play pranks with me. I'm well aware of what is going on between you two". Cynthia's piercing cry was heard by Mrs and Mr Williams and they walked fast towards the bedroom. They tried to push the door but Eshan was not ready to listen, he had bolted the door from inside. They told him to stop thrashing Cynthia but to no avail. Two to three minutes passed and suddenly there was a grave silence. Soon, Eshan pushed open the door. Mrs and Mr Williams entered the room to see Cynthia lying in a pool of blood. She screamed, "You scoundrel, how dare you hit this innocent girl?! Leave my house, right now! Nathan had come to invite us to his marriage. Cynthia my child, I'll call the ambulance."

Cynthia lay in the ICU of St. George Hospital. Mrs William and Mrs Brown stood sobbing near the glass door to have a look at their most adorable child. The Doctor came up to them and said in a heavy voice, "We want to tell you clearly that her condition is stable and we have to do a C-Section as soon as possible. We'll try to save both the mother and child but rest is in the hands of the Lord." Mrs Brown was astonished to hear all the bitter truths and the hidden sufferings. She rebuked Mrs William for being so unscrupulous. It took four hours for Dr Verma's wife to complete the operation. She came out at five in the evening from the operation theatre holding a little bundle of joy. Coming up to the two ladies, she said in an ecstatic tone, "It's a boy and Cynthia is out of danger."

Ronnie came straight from school, caught hold of his mother's sari and started crying, "Mom, even I want to visit the School Fair. All my friends are going today. Why can't I go?" Cynthia had no answer to certain questions that Ronnie asked. Life was an arduous task for a single parent.

Ronnie, her ten-year-old had grown up with his mother. She remembered the day when she had reached Kolkata. It was a fifteen hours tiresome journey by road. Cynthia held her three-weeks old child in her arms and admired his round face, soft brown hair; well-shaped pink lips and dreamy eyes just like his dad.

Mrs. Brown accompanied her and made her settle down in the nurses' hostel in the New Market area. Both Mrs Brown and Mrs Williams didn't want Cynthia to live a life full of worries. A new woman had been born. That night she had innumerable questions to ask God.

Cynthia started working in the City Hospital and she earned enough money to bring up her son. The past life was a forgotten chapter. One night, late at around 1 a.m, she woke up suddenly as the call bell of her bedroom rang. The hostel-in-charge was standing outside; she spoke breathlessly, "Madam there is an urgent phone call for you from Darjeeling". Cynthia gathered her nightgown and rushed to take the call. On the other side was Rita who took care of Blessings. She spoke in a worried tone, "Madam, Mrs. Brown has had a heart attack, she is quite serious. She is uttering only your name repeatedly". Cynthia couldn't control herself. Tears rolled down her cheeks.

The next morning, she hired a taxi and left for Darjeeling. A decade had passed and she was taking Ronnie back to the most beautiful place on earth.  On the way, she had to answer his incessant questions. Late in the evening on reaching Darjeeling, she went straight to the hospital. Mrs. Brown was in the ICU of the same hospital in which she lay half-dead ten years back.

She couldn't control her tears on seeing Mrs Brown's condition. The lady had been her guiding light since birth. She had diligently handled all the vicissitudes of Cynthia's life. She was her Godmother. The doctor advised Cynthia to visit the next morning as Mrs Brown was fast asleep due to the heavy dose of medicines. She left the hospital and reached 'Blessings' late at night.

Early next morning she left for the hospital. Mrs Brown was lying on the bed with eyes wide open. It seemed as if she was waiting for Cynthia. She could make out from her gestures as if she wanted to say something. She called the doctor and Mrs. Brown indicated the oxygen mask. The doctor removed it slowly.  She quickly sat on the stool kept next to the bed.

Mrs Brown said in a grieved tone, "Cynthia my darling…. I'm happy you have come…I have been living with this pain in my heart since the day you left… In these ten years, I hid so many things from you… Mrs and Mr Williams died in an accident last year. Mrs Williams was my real sister but we were not on talking terms for years until the day she came with the marriage proposal. I wanted you to become a woman of substancc. Eshan is all alone now. Since the day you left, every single day he came to me to know about your whereabouts. The time has come now when you have to take over your two responsibilities, Eshan, and Blessings." After saying these words, Mrs Brown slipped into a deep coma. The same evening, she died.

Around six-thirty that evening, when the doorbell rang, Eshan was laying the plates for dinner. Wondering who had appeared so soon, he frustratedly went to the door. It was Nathan and he said excitedly, "I'm here to help you out…. stop being jealous of me from now onwards." Holding forward a single rose that had a long, slender stalk, he handed it to him. "Congratulations…. your wait is over…your love is returning…. Cynthia is coming back to you with your child Ronnie," Eshan thought that maybe the bygones were bygones for all now.

At seven-thirty in the evening, the gate flung wide open and Ronnie came rushing towards the door. Cynthia stood in the middle of the gate watching her Cherry Blossoms blooming with beautiful pink flowers. The soothing air and the sweet fragrance of the flowers seemed so welcoming. The intoxicating flowers symbolized renewal and it proved true that evening. Eshan stood in the middle of the door with arms stretched towards them. Nathan stood next to him with a few close friends. Cynthia had no questions left for God that day.

# To Payal With Love

"Doctor, please examine my baby…. it's turning blue…she is unable to breathe," cried Mihika as she came running breathlessly to the doctor. He made the half-conscious infant lie down on the hospital bed, took out the stethoscope and called out, "Nurse come fast, bring the injection." Dr Abhinav Gupta, a famous paediatrician at the Government Hospital, Kanpur made the baby lie down on the stretcher in his room and patted its cheeks.

"How old is the baby?" asked the doctor examining the child.

She spoke with tears in her eyes, "Three days old …. she was born on the morning of 25th October in a private hospital…she was not keeping well…but see she can't breathe normally…our Doctor is unavailable."

The nurse handed him the injection and the Doctor injected the baby. The infant gained little consciousness and Mihika held her in her arms. The child did not cry and she held her close to her bosom. The doctor signalled Mihika to sit on the bench and said, "The child has some major complications. You will have to go for further check-ups to Delhi Government Hospital. They have experienced doctors and proper facilities. I will write a letter to the doctor at the hospital in Delhi. What is the child's name?" asked the doctor.

"Payal…. I have named her Payal Malhotra," said Mihika with a faint smile holding her close to her heart.

The coming days were hectic for the family as the doctors in Delhi admitted her for a week and the regular check-ups were done. The reports were not satisfactory. The doctor called Mihika one morning and said, "Madam your daughter is suffering from a serious heart disease called Atrial Septal Defect and she needs to be operated on as soon as possible".

Baby Payal was operated and stayed in the ICU for a month. Mihika prayed day and night for her child and was happy on the day she was discharged.

They returned to their home teary-eyed with the Doctor's advice, "Baby Payal is better now but you will have to come for regular check-ups every three months. Her medicines and check-ups will continue life-long. You will have to keep in mind that she doesn't fall seriously sick because her heart is weak. If any serious complication arises it will be difficult for us to save her."

Payal started growing up as a normal child but her medication and regular monthly check-ups had to continue till her heart became normal. She was admitted to a local school a bit late than other children. She was a brilliant child and would easily make friends. As Payal was over age compared to the rest of her class, most of her classmates looked younger than her.

The new session began in April. In Grade 6 she met Sameer. He was a quiet child always sitting in one corner without any friends. For fifteen days she had been noticing Sameer sitting on his bench alone in the interval.

One day in the interval she went up to him said, "Hello I'm Payal…..and your name is…....?"

"Sameer….my name is Sameer…. Hello… Payal," he spoke getting up from his seat and keeping the biscuit back in the tiffin.

"See I'm a bit…. grown-up…. I feel awkward."

He started blushing and said while closing the tiffin, "Can we become friends…...even I am new…I am not good in studies…. I have nobody to help me at home in my studies."

They shook hands and Payal said sweetly, "From today we are best friends…. I can help you in your studies…. if you want."

The bell rang and they rushed towards the class. When the school was over, they exchanged their landline telephone numbers.

Payal would often go to Sameer's house to help him in his studies. Mr Anurag and Mrs. Vinita Sharma were pleased to see this and they were happy that their introvert son had finally found a friend. Payal's parents also supported their daughter and accepted their friendship.

Years flew by and it was the greatest moment of Payal and Sameer's lives as they passed their Intermediate with flying colours. Standing in the school premises Sameer ran up to Payal with her computerized mark sheet and said, "All this is possible because of you…my first intelligent friend…. wise…I remember the first day I met you…. I was an average child…. but you… even though you were on medicines…. you kept guiding me…and today I stand with such a brilliant result…. unexpected. Thank You, Payal."

Payal was smiling while listening to all this and she said taking her mark sheet from him, "Sameer, I am grateful to God for giving me the strength to help you out in your studies…we have done it…. now we will go our separate ways…. I will be staying in my city and continuing with my passion of dress designing. What about you?"

"I'll be going to Delhi….to continue with my BBA and then MBA. Five years is a long period…. staying away from my parents….and a good friend."

She moved forward with him towards the car and they drove off. Five years passed and Sameer kept coming home during his vacations. They would spend time at their local Coffee House. He would order his favourite Cold Coffee with Vanilla Ice-cream while she loved to drink her Mint Iced tea. They had grown up together, studied together and they had their highs and lows together. Their relationship was as pure as the driven snow. Payal looked thin and delicate as the doctors had advised her to continue with her medicines lifelong. She still pretended to look strong and confident.

After five years, Sameer was back to start a business with his family. His father owned a small land in the city and he wanted to set up a school. He began the project soon and Payal was always there to help him out. They did practically all the discussions together and he found himself at ease with Payal. They named the school 'The Wordsworth School' and it began in the new session.

One evening while at dinner Mr Anurag told Sameer, "Sameer, now that you have started with your new venture, I would like you to settle down in your life."

"Oh, dad you can wait for a few months…. let the school run smoothly…. I am not ready for marriage," he said holding his father's hand.

"My friend Shivraj has a beautiful daughter and she has just returned from Mumbai after completing her English Honours. He wants you to meet her daughter as he is interested in making you his son-in-law…... can I fix for a meeting in a day or two?"

"No, dad…. please wait…I've got to talk to you…. though I never discussed earlier."

His mother spoke lovingly, "You can tell us Sameer…...any special girl in your life…. tell me."

"Mom and Dad, I want to marry Payal…. I haven't asked her yet… but she has been the closest to me for years."

Anurag got up from his chair with anger and said, "That's impossible…how can you even think of that…she is suffering from a serious heart ailment…. since years…. I believe lifelong…you can't have a secure future with her…. I will not take any risk."

"Please, Dad…. you are well acquainted with my behaviour…. I feel more at ease with her…. you should give this a second thought," Sameer said and moved towards his room.

Mr and Mrs Sharma knew that their son was adamant and discussing this matter with him was like talking to a brick wall. They decided to pay a visit to Payal's house the coming Sunday.

Mr Anand and Mrs Mihika Malhotra welcomed them.

"Namaste…How are you?" greeted Anand as they sat in the living room.

"Mr Malhotra, I will not take much of your time…. I have come to talk about Payal."

"Is everything okay? Should I call her?"

"No… no… Sameer wants to marry Payal."

Anand couldn't speak a word. Finally, he spoke with his eyes wide open, "Anuragji…please…you know about her health…. she has to take medicines lifelong…. she can't bear a child…. none of the boys will adjust….it may create differences in future…. I love my daughter…I have nobody else."

The two couples decided to talk to their children and the next Sunday was fixed for it. Sameer had never talked about marriage to Payal. He knew deep down in his heart that Payal would never agree but he could never accept any other life partner in his life. She was his first and last choice.

The next Sunday the two families met and Payal sat with Sameer to discuss this sensitive issue.

Sameer began, "Uncle and Aunty…. I respect you and today I want your daughter's hand in marriage…. I know everything about her…her illness…her strengths…her weaknesses…her likes and dislikes…I am more comfortable with her…you can take Payal's approval."

Payal said in a serious tone, "Sameer, we have been good friends but we can never become husband and wife. My illness will follow me and I can never fulfil your wishes of becoming parents. You should choose some other girl…. please…. please…it is a request."

Sameer became quite serious, "Payal, a man and woman can become life partners without conditions of parenthood. There are so many orphanages lying in the world with children who need parents. I have no objection to adopting a child…. but I need you at every step of my life…. Please don't refuse…Payal."

Payal couldn't say no to him and both the families congratulated each other. The marriage was fixed on the 16th of November 2013. Payal looked enchanting in her mahogany bridal wear and Sameer looked striking in his white suit. It was a grand celebration and their parents stood content at their choice.

Early in the morning, Payal was welcomed to her new abode by her in-laws. Sameer's dream had been fulfilled. Sitting next to her while the rituals were being performed, he said, "Payal, I think you need to take care of yourself and your medicines…. where have you kept them."

"In the black carry bag."

He told the servant to carry her luggage to their room. He took her to their room, opened the bag and took out the medicines. He embraced her and made her sit on the chair. He kissed her forehead then handed her the box of medicines. She took them out and placed them on the bed side table. Sameer poured water into the glass and handed it to her. She gulped down her medicines.

He caught hold of her hand and took out a small pouch from his pocket and handed it to her. He said, "This is a small token of love…. this is the happiest day of my life….my life is sitting in front of me…. I am with you through thick and thin…. I want you to take care of yourself rather than me and my family."

Payal opened the gift and took out the gold anklets and opened her eyes wide, "Beautiful…. Sameer….so pretty…I love them." She handed them to him and put her feet forward. Sameer wore her anklets and she loved her feet with them. He said, "I wanted to gift you this for so many years…. something special…...related to your name…...now you better take some rest…must be tired." He made her lie on the bed and switched off the light.

The house was brimming with enthusiasm and laughter as it was the 16th of November 2019. Three cakes were arranged on the table and the first cake was written,' 'Happy Birthday Poppy', on the second was written, 'Happy Birthday Sammy' and on the third, 'Happy Anniversary Payal and Sameer'

Sameer and Payal were celebrating their sixth anniversary as well as the birthdays of their children. Poppy a stunning, grey-eyed girl with short hair had turned five and Sammy their son was three. They had adopted them from the orphanage. They were satisfied they had given name to two beautiful creations of God. They wanted the world to learn that childless parents should go for adoption. Let these children also have a home.

The Coronavirus had spread in the country and the doctor was regularly telling Payal to be extra careful. In October 2020, Payal went with her mother for a regular check-up to Delhi. They reached at ten in the morning. On reaching Delhi she fainted at the airport and was rushed to the hospital. Her mother called up her husband and Sameer. The country was going through a very bad phase. She was admitted with major heart complications to the hospital. The virus was attacking people with low immunity and those suffering from serious ailments. The doctors tried their level best but could not save her. She couldn't even say a final goodbye and entered a new world without Sameer. She left two beautiful souls to be nurtured and taken care of.

# Love Will Cross Boundaries

After a hectic day, Sophia returned from her office. It was seven in the evening when she rang the bell with her elbow, as she was holding two heavy bags full of grocery. It was Friday and, on the weekend, practically all the stores were closed. It was dark outside with the temperature dipping to -1 degree. She wanted to relax and stay cosy in her bed on weekends.

She called out, "Kia…. open the door…. Kia."

A fair-complexioned girl, almost twelve years of age and with small eyes, opened the door. Seeing her, Sophia asked in a worried manner, "Where were you, Kia….my baby…just hold these." She handed her one packet and kept the other one on the kitchen platform.

"What will you have for dinner? Should I prepare some chicken noodles?"

"Yes, mom…. Did you get my strawberry chocolates? I told you," Kia spoke checking the packets.

"Of course," she said emptying them. Then, she switched on the burner to prepare her coffee as she had to sit down and complete some pending work of the office. The two-room flat was sufficient for them; she sat on the chair and placed her laptop on the dining table. She opened it to check her emails and her hands started trembling. The mug almost fell from her hands and she spilt some hot coffee on her clothes.

"Oh…. Oh my God."

Kia was noticing her and she came running, "What happened, mom?

"Nothing…. there is such a lot of work to be completed today…. I got confused."

Kia hugged her tightly and said, "Mom…. leave some for tomorrow."

"No, my child ….it will hardly take an hour…. then I will prepare dinner." She was happy to have such a caring daughter. She was her heart and soul and she knew she was alive just for her sake.

The e-mail that shook her read,

"My sweetheart Sophia…. I'm back….it has been twelve years and I was missing you. You belong to me, only me…see you soon."

Love of my life,

Only yours

Kabir

Sophia caught hold of her mug and fond, irreplaceable memories started flashing in.

It was the month of April when Sophia and her family landed at the Srinagar airport. Her parents Jennifer and Thomas Wendell had been married for twenty-five years and it was their silver jubilee on the 14th of April 2005. Sophia wanted to celebrate the silver wedding anniversary in India as it was a favourite tourist destination for the English. Mustafa greeted them at the airport and took them in a van to Dal lake. On the way, they were mesmerized on seeing the scenic beauty of Srinagar. The hills, valleys and the row of houseboats looked enchanting. They sat in a boat and reached their houseboat 'Mumtaz'.

It was a completely new experience for them. They settled themselves in their respective rooms. Sophia and her parents went for a short nap after lunch. Their cook Rizwan knocked into their room at 5 p.m. for tea. He served tea in the small garden situated on the left side of the houseboat. In a few minutes, they were joined by Mr

Mohsin Khan, the owner of the houseboat.

"Welcome…. Welcome to Kashmir sir…. happy to see you…... your arrangements have been done accordingly. What is the celebration tomorrow?"

The Wendell's greeted him and Sophia began with excitement, "Well, tomorrow is my mom and dad's silver anniversary. I would like you to arrange a small party…. we can invite the two families staying in the adjoining house-boat and of course, your family too. We want a lunch party as mom and dad will be leaving for Pahalgam for three days."

"Madam, all the arrangements will be done according to your choice and my son will be organizing everything. Anything else, madam?"

"I want a beautiful anniversary cake too…please see to it."

"Sure ma'am…good evening…my son will meet you in the morning."

The next morning, Sophia made a beautiful bouquet with fresh flowers and knocked her parent's room.

She embraced her mother, handed her the bouquet and said, "Oh mama…Happy Anniversary…. may you have many more years of togetherness" and moved to wake up her dad, "Good morning dad, Happy Anniversary…. wake up."

After having her bath and morning tea, Sophia wore a pair of jeans and a white shirt and moved towards the garden to oversee the preparations. She stood there looking at the boats sailing in the lake with girls in their traditional dresses selling flowers, fruits and vegetables. The sight was breath-taking.

"Madam…madam…. good morning," wished Kabir.

She turned back to see an extremely fair complexioned, tall, decent man standing in his blue jeans and full sleeves warm red shirt.

"Hello! Good Morning."

"I'm Kabir….my dad must have told you yesterday."

"Yes…I'm Sophia……it's my parents silver jubilee and I want the place to be decorated in white and silver with fresh flowers. You can get a small music system too…. I hope you have ordered the cake."

"Madam, have full faith in us. I will get everything done by twelve…. leave it to me…. I will do my best."

By twelve, Sophia was ready in a pink gown with high heels and her favourite diamond studs. She reached the drawing-room where her parents were already waiting. Her mother looked graceful in her silver gown with a diamond and pearl necklace, while her father looked handsome in his grey suit with a red tie.

"Mom and dad, you both look fabulous…. love you," screamed Sophia. "Let's go…Kabir, the owner's son, had given assurance that he will do the best."

Sophia walked with her parents to the venue. She stood awestruck and gazed at the entrance gate which looked classy with white roses and silver ribbons. Two Kashmiri girls stood there singing their traditional song to welcome them. As they entered, she saw all around that the small garden had been transformed. The neatly arranged tables, with one in the centre with the cake and silver-white balloons, glistened with the sunrays peeping from the clouds.

The two families with the owner's family had a gala time. Sophia sang a melodious song for her parents and after the cake cutting, they danced to their favourite song. The food was equally delicious and they relished the Kashmiri cuisine. Sophia wanted to thank Kabir but he was nowhere to be seen.

She went to Mohsin and asked, "I loved every bit of it….it was more than what I had thought of…. I would like to thank your son."

"Thank you, madam…. he has gone for some urgent work…. you can meet him in the evening."

In the evening by six, Sophia's parents left for Pahalgam. She came back to her room, took a warm bath and wore her woollen black night wear.

There was a knock at the door and she went to open it.

"Madam…. Kabir sir is here…. waiting outside."

"I'm coming in a minute."

She, rushed as she wanted to meet Kabir and thank him. Kabir greeted her and couldn't take his eyes off her as she looked stunning in black with her hair open.

He handed gave a small gift pack and said, "Madam I couldn't be there but this is for your parents…. a token of love…. something from Kashmir…. heaven on earth."

She went with him to sit outside and ordered coffee. She loved his black dress and the embroidered shawl.

"Thanks…. but…we had a great time… I loved the flowers, cake…...everything….it was the most precious day for my parents and I am happy they loved it."

She didn't even realise how she fell into deep conversation with him. They enjoyed the coffee and while he was about to go, she asked him, "Tomorrow I will be going to visit the historical gardens. Can you accompany me if you have time? Otherwise, I will manage…. I don't know if it is safe to go alone."

"Madam, we have arranged a good driver…. but I am free tomorrow…see you at ten in the morning."

Sophia was ready at nine in a yellow warm dress and was sitting in the sun reading the newspaper when Kabir called her, "Madam…. I'm ready…we can go now." She was getting attracted to his sober looks, generosity and capability. She had started liking his company although she knew nothing about him.

They visited the famous gardens and clicked photographs. She enjoyed lunch at a famous restaurant situated on a hill top. It was a fabulous day for her and she noticed the other aspects of him as he was full of the joys of spring.

It was almost seven when they returned in a boat. Sophia was already tired when the small boat reached 'Mumtaz'. Kabir got down quickly and Sophia followed him. He was climbing the stairs when he heard, 'Help! . please…. oh…uhm". He, turned back and jumped down the stairs and caught hold of Sophia's hand. She had slipped and fallen in the water but in the meantime the oarsman threw himself forward and held the boat with one hand and Sophia's hand with the other. Kabir gently pulled Sophia; she had tears rolling down her cheek. Her dress was wet, stained and she was shivering. Kabir engulfed her and made her stand straight.

He said standing close to her, "I think you are not having any problem in walking…Madam, God saved you today…Allah saved you….in this darkness if any mishap took place I would have become an imbecile for the rest of her life…... come…please." He took her to her room and opened the door.

"Madam…you can change. I am bringing the medicine."

Sophia went straight to the washroom and took a hot shower. She kept on wondering that what would have happened if she drowned. If Kabir hadn't saved her. She could feel his body next to hers. He was her saviour. Kabir ordered the cook to prepare some hot soup. Sophia dressed in her white nightwear and sat on the bed.

"Madam, can I come in?" someone asked in a thin voice. Sophia, still sitting in pain said, "Yes, the door is open." A diminutive pretty girl entered with an ointment and tablets. She came forward and said,

"Madam I will apply…I sister." She gently applied it on her ankle and left. The cook brought soup to her room. Kabir knocked the door, "Madam…Can I?"

"Of course. please come in."

He looked handsome in his traditional white dress with a fawn-coloured shawl.

"I hope you are feeling better," he asked her and she simply nodded her head. He got the dinner laid in the room and on her request, had dinner with her. He gave her the medicines and left the room.

The next morning her ankle was still paining and she slithered up to the dining room to have tea. Kabir came after breakfast and she requested him to arrange for a doctor. The doctor arrived after an hour.

He examined her ankle and said, "Madam, you have sprained your ankle so you are advised three days complete rest. I am writing the medicines which are to be taken regularly."

Sophia had no one to talk to except Kabir. He left for his work but agreed to have dinner with her. She passed the entire day reading her favourite novels. Dinner was arranged in the same manner but the cook tried to prepare something of her choice. She had something missing the whole day…. maybe Kabir…was it love or just infatuation…. she couldn't define it.

Kabir was in his jeans and overcoat as the weather had turned bad and it was raining outside. They talked, laughed and ate. Sophia had started liking his company. It was almost eleven when he got up to leave.

"Can you please pass me my medicines…they are in the drawer," she said.

He got up to open the drawer and handed her the medicines. He poured water into the glass for her. She sat and admired his every action. Something was pulling her to him a magnet. Was she in love with him?"

The moonlight was entering from the glass window which made the atmosphere calm and more soothing. She made herself comfortable on the bed and said, "Please switch off the light. good night."

Kabir switched off the light and was about to open the door when he heard Sophia moaning with pain. He moved towards her and asked her, "I hope you are well."

"My ankle is aching. don't worry."

He was standing very close to her bed. She caught hold of his hand when he tried to leave.

She urged him, "Can you sit for a few minutes. please?"

She wanted him to sit with her and spend some more time. She pulled him and he almost fell on her. She knew she wanted him although it was against caste, creed, and culture. She was lying close to him; she embraced him and whispered in his ears, "I am falling in love with you."

He stood up to leave and said, "Madam I think it's doesn't seem to be good….you are our guest."

Sophia wanted him anyhow because she could feel something pulling her to him. She made him sit on the bed and kissed his hand, "I don't know Kabir…if this relationship continues or not but…. my heart beats for you, I long for you."

She pulled him down took his hands and placed it on her waist. She said softly, "Please….it is only between you and me."

He kept holding her and said, "If this a beginning of friendship, then it has to stay…. I can never express my feelings because I know such relationships have no future…. you will always stay in my heart….

if it happens…I won't leave you…we will give it a name…. I respect women…. I don't want to be called a betrayer…. if you don't mind, I'll take your leave…it's almost midnight."

She was the first one to make a move and she started, "No Kabir…. I agree with you." She kissed him and she pulled him on the bed. He made love to her and left after an hour.

She had one more day with him as her parents had not yet returned. She waited for him in the morning but he didn't turn up. The cook informed her that he will be back by evening. She stayed in her room till seven in the evening. At eight, there was a knock at the door and she replied, "Please come in…it's open."

Kabir entered with a gift pack. He handed it to her and said, "I hope you like it. please open."

She opened the packet and took out the black shawl. "It's beautiful I love it."

After dinner she said, "Mom and dad will be back tomorrow…I can talk to them about. our new love story."

"My parents are very broad minded. I am their only son…. they always have faith in me."

She walked slowly up to him and embraced him. He had fallen in love with a woman who expressed her love first and made him fall head over heels in love with her. They made love without any regret.

She woke up the next morning on hearing a commotion. She got down from her bed, wore her slippers and rushed outside. She caught hold of the chair on seeing the terrible scene. There were more than fifty policemen with guns holding Kabir and his father. One of them shouted, "You scoundrels. both father and son…cheaters."

The two other senior officers moved forward and one of them shouted, "You thought we won't come to know. deceivers…you will stay behind the bars lifelong."

She stood stupefied with tears rolling down her cheeks. "How could she be so innocent…naïve…. falling in love…. unknowingly…. with a bleak future ahead."

A week passed with Sophia's ears always alert with the fear of hearing a knock from him. She had already told Kia not to open the door or talk to strangers. A month passed and she had somewhat forgotten about the mail when one morning, on the last Sunday of the month, there was a gentle knock at the door. The doorbell rang and she left the pan on the gas stove with the scrambled eggs almost cooked, to open the door.

Sophia looked pretty even after so many years in her blue dress. She said with her face almost white, "Oh no…. I knew…you will find me…. but…. please come…I hope everything is safe and sound."

Kabir looked a bit thin, worn out but striking in his black overcoat. He sat in the living room and Kia entered to see the stranger. He called her close and they started talking. Sophia brought coffee and cookies for him. She sent Kia inside as she had never told her about a man in her life. Kabir had so many things to tell her, so he began quickly, "Sophia…. I hope you are fine. Thirteen years have passed…. I know you must have settled down…you have a beautiful daughter…but I wanted to meet you."

"Why… Kabir…. after all these years… I don't need any clarifications…. everything was quite clear…. it was in the newspapers…. television…. everywhere. Why did you hide? I shouldn't have fallen in love."

"You have to believe… it was all false… they released us but not our passports…. I got the permission to leave the country two months back."

"How can I believe all this?"

"You have to. I would like to meet your husband and take leave…. my mind is finally free…I have told you the truth…I didn't marry because I was committed…you will always be my first and last love."

Sophia got up from the sofa and sat next to him. She caught hold of his hand and said, "After all these years…. I am at ease…I thought I had fallen in love with the wrong person. But maybe I was wrong."

Kabir longed for this touch and he said, "I am happy that you are settled."

Sophia said putting her head on his shoulder, "Kabir, you are the only man in my life…. I was so upset that time, and then we left the very next day. When we returned to London, I came to know that I was carrying your child…I told my parents…. they got angry and forced me to abort the child but I knew our bond was strong…Mom and Dad died in an accident after a year…. they had accepted her as their grand-daughter… Kia is your daughter…. her name bears it… K from Kabir and 'ia' from Sophia…. somewhere deep down in my heart I knew you would come back."

Kabir's eyes were filled with tears and he hugged her tightly, "Oh my God…. Sophia… Kia is the most precious gift… I'm so happy… I love you…. you are the best part of my life…. destiny brought us together years ago…I came across for you…. I knew for my love I could cross boundaries. I love you, Sophia."

# *Jasmine*

It was ten o'clock when Sanchita entered her daughter's bedroom. She opened the door by pushing it with her elbow as her hands were occupied with a bunch of roses in one and a small gift pack in the other.

"Hello, darling. my child Jassi…. Jasmine."

She found the bedroom empty so she went up to the washroom and knocked  the door.

"Jasmine. are you inside…happy birthday baby?"

There was no answer; so, she came up to the bedside table to free her hands when suddenly her eyes caught sight of a letter placed under the coffee cup. There was an envelope too placed on it. She picked up the letter and started reading.

"My Dear Mum and Dad,

I'm eighteen today and by the time you read the letter, I will be married to George Wilson in the court. It was in my mind for so many days but I couldn't gain the courage to tell you all. It is my decision so need not worry. I am taking my pocket money along with me. Take care of Love and Kush. I will miss you…. don't cry.

Love you,<br>Jasmine"

Sanchita could feel tears running down her cheeks and she rushed out of the room to inform Mohit.

"See Mohit…. see…... how could she…... such a fool she is," Sanchita said with her hands trembling as she handed the letter to

Mohit who was getting dressed up for the office. He started reading the letter and sat down on the chair in the bedroom. He placed his hands on his forehead and said, "Oh my God. Jasmine!! …...How could you…...shame on you."

They tried to connect with her on the mobile but it was switched off. Love and Kush loved their sister and couldn't make out what was happening in their house. Sanchita simply informed them that she had left the house as she had got a poor result but they were trying to get her back.

The knock at the door early morning at six o'clock startled Mohit. He quickly got up from the bed and wore his slippers. He reached the drawing-room and opened the door. He saw Jasmine standing outside thin with dishevelled hair. She was carrying a faded plastic bag. Mohit tried to close the door but she caught hold of his hand and fell at his feet. In these five years, they had stopped following her for they were threatened by the Wilsons. They were more powerful and Jasmine was on top of the world.

In these five years, she had understood the value of her parents. George was the son of her principal, an alcoholic and fully dependent on his parents. The newly married Jasmine tried her level best to adjust with his parents but in these five years, she failed desperately. She had been a brilliant student with many dreams. Her unfulfilled passions made her leave George and one fine morning, she decided to give life a fresh start. The only place left for her was her parent's house. She knew there would be rage and resentment but the love of parents is incomparable.

In the meantime, Sanchita too entered and caught hold of Jasmine by her shoulders tightly, "Why have you come back?"

With tears flowing down she said, "We have forgotten you…. you are dead for us…go back…. we are respectable people."

Jasmine hugged her mother sobbing continuously, "I am sorry, mom…. please…. where will I go…dad…I still love you…sorry… sorry."

Mohit stood speechless watching her. He came forward and said, "Jasmine…we still love you…...you have spoiled your future…. you didn't have faith in us…. we are still broken."

"I am not going back now…. I have realized my mistake…. I have been through hell…. he has ruined my life."

Mohit caught hold of her hand and brought her inside. She went with him straight to her brothers' room and stood there watching them. Then Mohit took her to her room and she was surprised to see that everything was kept in the same way as she had left.

"Daddy, I am sorry again…. I shouldn't have done this."

He started consoling her. In the meantime, Sanchita brought tea and biscuits.

"You take rest…we will never ask anything about your past…. you are beginning a new life from today…. let the bygones be bygones," Mohit said sitting next to Jasmine. After some time, he stood up and left the room.

Jasmine was fair complexioned, five feet six inches in height with long hair. George was attracted towards her from the very first day in college and after two years of courtship, they decided to elope. Innocent and decent Jasmine was lured by his talks and she dreamt of a blissful future ahead with him.

Love grows with experience. True love is rare, like searching for a pearl in the ocean. Love can happen at any time, at any age. It makes you commit serious mistakes at times.

Three years passed and George Wilson was a closed chapter of Jasmine's life now. After BBA, Jasmine got admission to the prestigious Government College for her MBA. She was divorced and trying to be back to her normal self now. She had lost faith in the institution of marriage; she still went into moments of depression.

"Jasmine, your cousin Rachna is getting married on the twenty-fifth and we will be leaving for Hyderabad on the twenty-first," Sanchita came up to her room and said in a hurry.

"Ma I can't go; I have my College…. please…. I can stay back."

"No…. your aunt will get angry…. you shall come with me to the market today and get two new dresses," said Sanchita pleadingly as she knew Jasmine was least interested.

They boarded the train from Delhi to Hyderabad on Saturday. It was raining heavily as it was the month of July. It took a day to reach and the weather was a bit humid. They were received by their aunt's family at the station. Raghavendra and Jasmine's cousin Rohan picked up the luggage and asked them to follow. They proceeded towards the cars and settled themselves. Raghavendra was introduced by Rohan as his school friend. Jasmine didn't speak much; she silently sat in the car with him.

The marriage preparations were going on and Raghavendra wanted to know more about this quiet girl. So, he went up to his friend in the evening and asked, "Rohan …. though you may feel bad…. but I want to know about this cousin of yours …. she doesn't speak much…. looks depressed."

"Raghavendra…. you are my best friend…. I can't hide from you her story…. she has suffered…. a lot…. now she is trying to settle down…. I want her to study…. I believe every mistake teaches you a lesson."

The marriage took place on Tuesday and Jasmine looked beautiful in a blue Lehnga (an Indian dress). Raghavendra couldn't take his eyes off her and tried his level best not to be attracted towards her but he wanted to know the hidden story. Mohit and Sanchita became very friendly with Raghavendra as he was handling half of the things in the marriage.

Mohit and Sanchita settled themselves for dinner with the two families after the marriage and Raghavendra ordered the waiters to get the dinner table laid.

"Uncle, you must try this special Hyderabadi dish made from vegetables and rice…Dum Biryani…. it's delicious," said Raghavendra to Mohit as he tried to pull the chairs for the bride and bridegroom. The bride Rachna was watching Raghavendra for the past three days so she told him to sit next to her. She started whispering to him, "Raghu… my brother…. I think you are in love."

"No Didi…. it's not so…. you are mistaken," he spoke almost blushing.

"I think you need to know more about Jasmine…...maybe after knowing the truth you won't take a step further…. you would look for somebody else."

When Raghavendra became free after the bride and bridegroom left, he came up to Rohan and said, "My curiosity and love is troubling me….do tell me. Can I talk to her parents?"

"You can …. but they won't agree…. Jasmine has decided not to marry…. you too will refuse after knowing the reality…. still, you can talk as they will leave for Delhi tomorrow."

In the evening when everybody gathered in the beautiful garden Rohan and Raghavendra came to sit with Mohit. Jasmine was seated in one corner with her brothers. She looked enchanting in a white salwar kameez and colourful dupatta. Raghavendra was falling more and more in love with her.

His hands were trembling and he began talking to Mohit, "Sir, though it doesn't seem to be good, I want to marry your daughter."

Mohit got up with a jerk from his chair and said, "How can you…. being so frank…. where are your parents….my daughter… Jasmine? Please."

Mohit had tears in his eyes and he called Sanchita who was gossiping with her relatives, "Sanchita…...see what is he asking for…. my son, you are an eligible bachelor…. Sorry…. don't think about her."

Saying this he went into his room with Sanchita. The atmosphere became so tense. They had never thought of her marriage as Jasmine was still trying to recover from her trauma. The bleak past was still walking behind her.

The next morning Raghavendra came up to them and said, "I'm sorry …. if I have hurt your feelings but please can I know the pain lying behind her sadness?"

Mohit narrated the traumatic story of Jasmine to him. Raghavendra sat motionlessly and caught hold of Mohit's hands and said, "I pity her…. but mistakes done should be pardoned….my problem is that I have fallen in love with her…. and I am ready to accept her…. she will never remember the dark days of her life… please, can you ask Jasmine for my sake?" Saying this, he left the room.

In the meantime, Jasmine entered wearing a simple dress. Mohit made her sit next to him and asked her, "Have you ever thought of marriage, Jasmine? We won't be living forever…...you have to decide someday."

"Dad, I told you three years back that I do not believe in the institution of marriage …. if you feel I am a burden on you…. I will soon start working…. but please don't force me," Jasmine replied somberly.

"Jasmine, have you met Raghavendra? He is a nice guy…I don't know much about him but you can give it a second thought…...do you want to meet him?"

"No dad…I'm not interested," she spoke stiffly.

All of them sat in the cars and reached the railway station. Their eyes met for a few seconds but Jasmine turned away her face and moved towards the train. They settled themselves and Rohan and Raghavendra moved forward to touch their feet.

Mohit patted their back and said, "God bless you"

✦ ✦ ✦

Three months had passed after that incident. One day, Rohan came for some urgent work to Delhi. After dinner that night Mohit, Sanchita and Rohan sat with coffee in the lobby when suddenly Rohan began the conversation as if he was waiting for it.

"Uncle…How is Jasmine? I hope she is doing well in her studies."

"Yes…. she has been a brilliant student always…. I am worried…. about her future."

"Raghavendra still wants to marry her…he has talked with his parents too…. he is now posted in Delhi…. he has decided to pass the rest of his life as a bachelor…. he will get married only to Jasmine… you can still talk to her."

"Rohan…I too want her to get married…. you can invite him tomorrow for dinner…. I'll talk to her."

The next evening Sanchita prepared a lavish dinner. Raghavendra got a bit late as Tilak Nagar was far from the cantonment.

Jasmine went to open the door and greeted him, "Good evening… please come in." She made him sit in the drawing-room and called her dad.

That day she had helped her mother in the kitchen as her father had told her in advance that she has to sit and talk with Raghavendra.

The final decision will be left to her. Mohit, Rohan and Sanchita made them sit in the adjoining bedroom. Jasmine looked pretty in blue jeans and a white shirt with her hair open. She sat on the chair next to him. She had noticed deep love in his eyes.

Raghavendra gathered courage and said in a low voice, "I shouldn't have come again…but in you, I see happiness, adoration and my future. I have heard about all the things that happened with you…. you have suffered …. but this is not the end of life…you have to live."

Tears started streaming down Jasmine's eyes. Raghavendra caught hold of her hand. She replied, "Oh…please leave me alone…. I have been used so many times…. How can you accept me with so many faults?"

"I am more interested in loving your soul than your body…. your past will be left far behind…. please don't refuse…. I love you."

Jasmine went speechless and couldn't utter a word. She stood up still holding his hand. Raghavendra wanted to pull his hand back but she held it tightly. Sobbing continuously, she moved towards him, hugged him tightly, and spoke softly, "I couldn't take this decision so quickly…... I have been tortured, beaten and thrown out….as if I was lifeless…. those moments keep haunting me day and night…. but your love is true."

He started wiping her tears and said, "I will stand with you…. you will never remember the dirty past…. we will live a new life full of the fresh fragrance of Jasmine flowers…my parents too will never come to know about your past…. they will accept you….as you are my choice."

After fifteen minutes, they both came out hand in hand and Jasmine rushed to her parents. Sanchita stood up and embraced her daughter as the smile on her face was an answer to her question. Mohit was very happy for his daughter and said, "God made marriages in heaven…. he knows what is best…. I have no words for the greatness and sacrifice of Raghvendra….my daughter is fortunate…. Thank you, Jasmine, for accepting him as your life partner."

Raghavendra came and sat next to Mohit and held his hand, "I am on top of the world and your efforts have proved to be fruitful…. but I would like to tell you something important."

On hearing this Sanchita and Rohan came and sat next to Raghavendra while Jasmine kept standing next to her two brothers.

"I want all of you to keep her first marriage a secret from my people.….my parents are orthodox and I know they will never agree.…... but I want to spend the rest of my life with Jasmine…you will have to tell your relatives too…. please, it is a sincere request…. living life long with such decisions is impossible, I know …. but for our sake."

He then continued saying, "It is your decision, not ours but I hope no difficulty arises in future…. you will have to handle it…. I don't want her to be a sufferer anymore."

The meeting with Raghavendra's parents was arranged in the coming week and they loved Jasmine from the moment they saw her. The date for marriage was fixed and they got a month's time for preparations.

On the fifteenth of November, Jasmine looked mesmerizing in her red wedding dress and Raghavendra awesome in his blue suit. He stood at the entrance door to welcome her.

Finally, he was holding her hand…. the hand he was longing for… the hand that he would hold till his last breath…. the hand of his love…the hands of the woman of his dreams: Jasmine.

# The Phulkari Dupatta

"Stop chasing that girl, I am warning you. Don't you dare spoil her name!" screamed Mangat Singh to his son Nishan.

"But dad, I am not the only one…. all my friends tease her…. I never tease…. she laughs at us….and threatens us," spoke Nishan in a shy manner with his eyes stuck in the ground.

"You are eighteen years old now. Old enough to join my jewellery business and get married. You know very well that her father is a police inspector…. all of you will be thrashed…get ready tomorrow morning by eight…. you are joining the family business from tomorrow." Saying this, Mangat Singh banged the door and left.

Eighteen years is the age of new love and infatuation. Since the day Nishan had seen Aagya at the Gurudwara, he kept dreaming about her. He never spoke a word but silently followed her with his friends. She admired this fair Sikh with ferocious eyes and a black turban. An unspoken love was blossoming between the two.

Every day, Nishan got ready at seven in the morning to follow Aagya. Full of pride with a thundering voice she made the boys more aggressive. Her shapely figure, sweet lips, and glossy skin made her look stunning. Every morning at seven, she went with her friends from her village to the local Gurudwara of Lahore. She ignored all the boys but had a special corner in her heart for Nishan.

Nishan Singh made a point to wake up at six and get dressed up by seven. The lane which Aagya crossed was at a distance of three kilometres. He cycled every day with his friends to that lane, followed her till the Gurudwara, and way back.

It was mid-July and dark clouds had gathered that morning. Nishan woke up as usual and despite the drizzle, he left for his daily cycling up to the Gurudwara. He had to return early that day as he had to reach his father's shop. He wore a white shirt with black pants and a turban. In half an hour he reached the lane and stood there waiting for Aagya and her friends.

He saw her coming and stood for a second as she looked a bit different, more pretty that day. As she crossed him, he got attracted to her white phulkari dupatta (stole) with colourful tassels. She was carrying it elegantly. As her dupatta flew with the wind, she looked more alluring.

He gathered courage that day and said, "Hello Madam…. something special…. tell me."

She simply smiled at him and moved forward. Three more bicycles came from nowhere and started following her. They were middle-aged men and one of them with curly black hair and dark complexion said, "Hello beautiful…....what a walk…lovely waist…hot…. come, darling."

"How dare you…. get lost…. you scoundrels!" shouted Aagya, her eyes burning with fire.

"You are the daughter of Inspector Santokh Singh…....a real bastard…. ruining our lives…. torturing Muslims…. we will soon have our own country."

"Don't you dare abuse my father…he is doing what is right."

"You…. you…bitch….we won't spare you….you,"said the tallest one in a fit of rage and caught hold of Aagya. The passers-by didn't stop and even the three girls walking with her, ran towards the Gurudwara. The six of them caught hold of her tightly and she tried her best to free herself.

"Leave me…. ooh…ummm…. you are hurting me…my dad won't leave you…leave," she cried on top of her voice. Nishan was silently watching all these bizarre happenings. He was a timid, introverted teenager doing what his young immature mind was pleased with. He gathered courage and rushed towards them but they pushed him down. They hit his legs badly with a thick wooden stick and moved forward.

"She will be punished for her dad's sins…...take her…. carry her," saying this one of them carried her on her back.

It started raining heavily and Nishan got up and rushed towards them as they carried Aagya towards the nearby fields. They continuously threw him down but he still tried to run holding his badly injured left leg. They threw her down in the thick bushes and two of them caught hold of Nishan. Aagya's shrieks were suppressed as one of them tightly pressed her mouth.

"Please leave her…. she is innocent…. leave her," pleaded Nishan, but not a single soul stirred. They threw her white dupatta and tore her clothes. He closed his eyes tightly and begged them to leave her, but nobody listened. One by one they bent down on her. Her cries had reached the sky above. She fainted and due to the incessant screeching, Nishan went into complete silence. They left after half an hour and Nishan rushed towards Aagya with her white stole. She was lying in meagre clothing, bleeding and almost dead. He took off his turban and covered her from top to toe. He was continuously wiping his tears and patting her cheeks but she did not gain consciousness.

In the meantime, the local police arrived. Two ladies ran towards Aagya and one of them fell on her, "Wake up my doll…. what happened….my daughter…. all of a sudden…we were planning to leave…take her to the hospital…...quickly."

The other lady covered her properly and two men from their family came forward and carried her to the police van. Nishan took the dupatta and rolled it like a turban. He too was taken to the police station.

The India Pakistan partition of 1947 brought bloodshed, chaos and migration. Practically all Non-Muslims had started moving towards India months before the partition. Some walked for several kilometres, others came on trains, buses and lorries. Some families reached with all their members safe while others reached alone as ladies and girls were either kidnapped or killed.

More than a hundred families had taken shelter in Refugee Camp number 1 in Amritsar. The tent houses were not in a good condition as the rainwater entered through the holes and the beddings became wet. On one side, the arrangement for food and water was done. The ladies gathered to cook vegetables, pulses, and chapatis. The badly injured ones were sent to another tent where a temporary hospital was set.

In one last corner of the hospital on a bed lay a young girl. Her parents and brother sat next to her. In between whenever she gained consciousness she started shrieking, "Kill them…. leave me…. call him…. please…please." The doctors gave her sedatives so that she slept. Her condition was worsening day by day and one night she started vomiting blood. Her brother rushed to the doctor's tent and called his parents.

"Your daughter is not trying to forget her past…. her condition is becoming worse day by day…. you will have to get her admitted to a government hospital," said the doctor and checked her pulse. Her mother Tara sat on the stool and wiped the drops of vomited blood from her face. She couldn't control herself and started sobbing. Her husband moved forward and caught hold of her.

The next morning there was a strange commotion as four to five people were running behind a young boy who looked mentally retarded. Finally, they caught hold of him and took him to the tent hospital. The doctor and compounder caught hold of him and tied him to the bed.

"Please see to him, doctor…. When will he become normal? He was such a good boy…. If I take this white dupatta from him, he starts hitting us…. he has been holding it for a month and a half…. he sleeps with it…. he eats with it…. he takes bath with it,"said Mangat Singh teary-eyed. "Nishan…my Nishan…. Waheguru save him." The doctor gave a syrup for Nishan and told his parents to be extra careful. He got the bed next to that girl.

In the evening Aagya opened her eyes and said, "Ma….ma…. water…thirsty." Her mother quickly poured water into the glass and brought it to her lips. Something strange was happening to her. She turned her head to see the bed next to her. Nishan was fast asleep. She stretched her hands towards him. Tara was watching all this but was unable to grasp the message she wanted to convey.

"My white…. rain…. white…. Nishan…. you," Aagya mumbled and Tara looked at him carefully. She went near to have a closer look and asked his dad, "Veerji (brother) I think she knows him…... where have you come from?"

"We are from Lahore…a terrible incident happened in his life…. since that day he hasn't left this white dupatta…. even I don't know the exact story behind."

"Even we are from Lahore…....my daughter too is suffering…. she was almost dead."

"These hooligans have spoiled the life of so many…. we have gained nothing from this partition…. except death and destruction."

Nishan lay unconscious the whole day as well as night. He woke up the next morning and tried to free himself. His father opened his cords and took him to freshen up. He was holding the white dupatta tightly and as he looked on the bed next to him, he stopped and called out, "Aagya…....you …….alive…....Aagya…....get up."

His father was shocked to hear such words from him. Aagya's mother too stood up from her place and exclaimed, "Should I wake her up…. maybe they know each other…may be Waheguru has brought them together."

Aagya opened her eyes and rubbed them to see the people surrounding her, "You…. where were you…that day…. day." She started crying loudly and Nishan started touching his white dupatta. He got very excited and started behaving abnormally. He showed it to her, "See…see…. I have it."

His parents failed to understand but Tara suddenly caught sight of the Phulkari dupatta. She ran towards it and opened it. The colourful tassels still hung on it with Aagya's name embroidered in one corner and she spoke hastily, "I made it for her birthday….it was a special day for her…she had turned seventeen…. see…her name is written on it…it was the darkest day of her life…. see her condition."

"This is my son Nishan…. he is the only witness to everything that happened that morning…...he hasn't recovered…...he is in shock…... we don't know what happened….it might have been a devastating sight…. I went to the police station to bring him back…. he keeps this dupatta close to him….at times says Aagya …... Aagya…we don't know about her," said Mangat Singh breathing heavily.

The two beds in the refugee hospital had two patients and both were witness to the gruesome results of partition. They were mentally unstable, feeble and still unknown about their whereabouts. Their love story had just begun but none of them knew what destiny had in store for them. They were now safe and secure.

Nishan and Aagya had a relaxed expression on their faces. He knew the bitter truth and she knew he would have still kept some secrets hidden in his heart. After a week, Aagya's condition started improving and her parents were relieved.

She was happy that her love was by her side. Their love was still not comprehended by their parents. Nishan too seemed to be content that she was alive and by his side. He had thought that she was dead. He was quieter and hardly spoke. He just lay on the bed and kept watching her with open eyes. He closed his eyes only while sleeping at night.

It took a month for Aagya to recover. One morning her parents started packing her things lying in the hospital. They came up to her and told her, "We are leaving for Delhi today as your dad has got a job…. we have taken your medicines."

Nishan was lying on his bed listening to all this. She wanted him to get up and stop her from going but due to his unsteady mental condition, he just kept staring at her. She didn't want to leave him. He had been her saviour and now she wanted to be his.

"Ma, I will not come with you…please," Aagya said sitting on his bed, tears flowing down and holding his hand. Mangat Singh and his wife came to her and said, "No Aagya, we are there for him…. don't worry…. he will get well soon…. he is recovering according to the doctor."

Tara and Sardar Santokh Singh who were standing next to their daughter came ahead and wiped her tears, "We will keep in touch and they will tell us once he gets well…. you have to equally take care of your health."

"No ma, you may leave…I will come…I have made up my mind that I will marry Nishan," she said and her mother caught hold of her shoulders and shrugged them. "No, my daughter…we love you…. we will marry you to a hale and hearty person…. you can't spend your life with him."

"Ma, I am the only one with whom he will spend his entire life…. his condition has improved…. because he loves me since the days, we grew up in Lahore…. he is the only one who will accept me with all my sins…. the immoral things that happened with me…. I will take care of him day and night…love can do wonders…. Waheguru has brought us together again."

Their parents were helpless and Aagya stayed back. Mangat Singh and his wife were more concerned about their son's health, so they accepted the proposal.

After two months Tara and Santokh Singh received a telegram and they left for Amritsar. They reached the huge house situated in Meena Bazaar. They were welcomed at the gate by Mangat Singh and his family. The scene inside made Tara hold her husband's hand tightly. He embraced her and moved forward. Their happiness knew no bounds on seeing Nishan tall, well built, dressed in a white kurta-pyjama and black turban.

The Haldi ceremony was being performed and Aagya was seated on a small wooden stool. Nishan came, took her parents inside, and made them sit on the chairs. He brought the beautiful Phulkari dupatta and wrapped it around Aagya lovingly. The tassels fell on her face. Aagya looked heavenly in the yellow dress. Their relatives were busy with the marriage preparations. The next day the marriage took place in the local Gurudwara.

That night Nishan came up to her and kissed her forehead and said, "I am alive because of you…. your dupatta had your fragrance….it made me feel your presence…. you sat by me night and day…. for you, I am back…. don't ever leave me now…. never in your life remember your horrid past…. our new life begins today."

# Who Killed Brinda?

"Siddharth.... Sid...dh...arth," someone called out. He woke up from his sleep, threw his quilt away, and almost jumped out of the bed. He turned around but no one could be seen. The door was shut and it was almost seven in the evening. As it was a weekend, there was less hustle bustle on the busy streets of Calcutta. The month of January of 2000 was colder than his previous seven years there.

The gentle tap at the door again startled him and again the same familiar voice could be heard, "Siddharth.... open Sidd....har..th"

He switched on the tube light and rushed towards the door, barefoot. He unbolted the wooden door and was surprised to see a young girl of seven to eight years standing with her parents. The girl looked cute in her pink woollen frock, stockings, and shoes while her parents were just like any other simple Indian parents. Her mother wore a green sari with a matching shawl, while her father wore a black sweater and pants with a muffler tied loosely around the neck.

"Yes ...how can I help you?" asked Siddharth looking at them from top to bottom.

"I am Roshan Sarkar and she is my wife Shalini…....my daughter…. Siddharth.... can we talk…. something urgent," said the man gracefully.

"How do you know my name?" he asked curiously "I have never seen you," said he.

"Can we come in….? We have come from Jaipur…we are facing a serious problem due to our daughter…. please listen to us."

"I don't allow strangers…. how can I believe that you have come to meet me?"

He was about to close the door when suddenly the small girl caught hold of his hand and he shuddered. Something strange happened and he asked her, "Who are you? …. you…. who…...leave!"

Siddharth thought that some black magic was being performed and he almost fainted. The couple caught hold of him and took him inside. He kept telling them, "Leave…. leave." The small girl came and sat next to him and started playing with his fingers.

He sat up and asked them, "Can I know the purpose of your visit…tell me soon…I am a bit uncomfortable."

"Tell him, Brinda…. come and sit with us and tell him…. come, Brinda."

Siddharth stood up and asked, "What is her name…. Brinda?"

He sat down and memories flashed in his mind. He was standing with his newly wedded wife at the threshold of his house in Jodhpur. His mother was doing the rituals and the bride gently pushed the brass pot full of rice with her feet. Siddharth had fallen in love with Brinda while working in a multinational company in Delhi. She was an orphan and lived with her aunt. They soon decided to get married. His family was quite supportive and they bought a small two-bedroom flat in Delhi. They moved to their new house, house number 23, and settled down well.

Every day, they left together for the office and Brinda returned an hour early. They knew nothing about their neighbours except that on weekends they tried to help the old lady Mrs. Sinha next door. She was the wife of a retired bank officer. Her husband died three years back and her only son could hardly be seen. She often told them about her past life and her notorious son. She gave blessings to both of them as they stood by her in times of trouble. A special relationship between mother and children developed in a few months.

He always thought that dreadful day should never have come to his life. He got a call in his office at six in the evening, "Siddharth babu…

please.…...come soon.…... I am the guard of your building."

"What happened? Please tell me," he said and the phone went down.

He threw his files, caught hold of his best friend Deepak, and sat on his bike to reach home. The building had twenty flats and two police vans were already there when he reached. He rushed towards his flat on the first floor and the scene was pathetic. Brinda was lying in minimal clothing full of blood. Siddharth fainted and the neighbours came forward to sprinkle water on his face. He gained consciousness and almost fell on Brinda when the policemen pulled him.

"Sir, it is a murder.…. your wife has been murdered.…...she was lying near the door…she struggled a lot…she is dead," said the inspector.

The whole universe seemed to be spinning as his love was lying dead in front of him. He was helpless; he shouted, howled but she was not coming back now.

"Why did God do this injustice? Who could have done this? Neither he had any enemies nor Brinda. How will he live without her? Was there a burglary? He is a widower now. Just six months of marriage and she left him alone and disturbed." All these questions kept whirling like a storm in Siddharth's mind.

The police sealed the house and his parents dropped in to console him but he had lost the love of his life. The investigations started but even after three months, the police were unable to find the murderer. Brinda was the most beautiful thing that had happened in his life. It was an unforgettable and incomplete chapter as the search for the murderer was still going on. He had not left a single clue.

Siddharth had already applied for a transfer and after three months, he got transferred to Calcutta. He locked that flat and moved to a rented house in Calcutta. Every night he sat in front of Brinda's photograph and told her about his daily engagements. She was his first and last love.

It had been seven and a half years now and even after his mother repeatedly sending new marriage proposals he refused blatantly. Suddenly a girl bearing the same name was standing in front of him, about to give strange explanations. He was sweating profusely in this chilly winter. This name was left only in his dreams.

"Yes….my child…...is there any special reason for you coming from Jaipur?" Siddharth asked anxiously.

"Siddharth …. she is my daughter…...born on the 10th of July 1992…. midnight."

The date seemed familiar to him but he preferred to remain silent. He wanted to hear from them.

"Since the day she learnt to speak…. she spoke strange words…. we named her Shambhavi but she kept muttering Brinda…. Brinda…... she was happy when we called her by this name. One fine day, she fell and got hurt and blood was oozing out from her toes…. when suddenly she started shouting…. "leave me…...leave me…. help" …. we were so surprised as there was nobody around."

"How can I believe in these made-up stories…. please don't think I am a fool…. you can leave."

"No, my son." The other day she came up to me and said, "Take me to Delhi… we have no one in that city…. she can write alphabets and numbers…. she wrote House number 23…. still, we could not understand. We knew nothing about all this until one day she told us about Jodhpur. She remembered your house well and last week, I went there. Your parents gave me your phone number and address…... I told them some other reason for meeting you…. Brinda wanted to see you…. she kept repeating your name…. I was not ready for all this but she is my only daughter…... I love her and care for her…. No one will understand this except you and us…. please help us."

The memories of house number 23 were still fresh and horrifying. He gave a strange look to the small girl who was listening to all these talks. He could see a reflection of Brinda in her now but maybe he was hypnotized. He pinched himself to feel his warm body.

He was in a dilemma as he had never come across such happenings in reality. It seemed more of a tale told by a grandmother. Suddenly, Siddharth stood up and said, "You can leave now…. you could have gathered this information from anywhere….it had come in the newspapers…. don't think of blackmailing me…...go."

Seven-and-a-half-year-old Brinda was listening to all these conversations quietly. She got up from her father's side and came and sat next to Siddharth.

"Please Sid…I remember everything…. should I begin?"

Only Brinda had called him Sid and her way of talking and expressions matched his Brinda's.

How was this possible!? He wanted her to speak.

"On the 9th of July, you left for the office on time and I came back early. As I saw the old lady's house was open, I peeped in and called out to her but no one could be seen. I unlocked our door and went again to see her. In the meantime, someone entered our house." She was speaking with such confidence that Siddharth got completely lost in her talk.

"How do you know all this? Who are you? Brinda is dead…. I cremated her myself…. I felt her dead body before setting it on fire," saying this, Siddharth started crying loudly.

The small girl continued, "As I entered the kitchen to prepare tea, I could sense someone standing behind me…... I turned around…... I tried to push him but he was quite hefty…I ran to my bedroom and tried to lock the door but he threw it open. I kept asking him…... Who are you?...... Why have you come?...... I don't know you…take all the things you want…....spare me…. but he started tearing my clothes…. somehow, I reached the main door…....I tried to open it but he slit my throat…. and then, ran away."

Siddharth got down on his knees in front of her and held her hands. He started sobbing and Brinda too started crying loudly. Her mother and father ran up to her and wiped her tears. "Can you recognize that person?" asked Siddharth. She gently nodded her head.

"Siddharth…she didn't tell us …...all these things…. maybe she remembered on seeing you…. we even took her to a psychiatrist…but he too wanted her to see you…they believe that maybe she will forget these incidents with the growing years…she was adamant to see you."

Siddharth was already in a state of shock and the clock struck 10. They were sitting without any water or tea. All of them were so engrossed in these somewhat authentic talks that hunger and thirst were far away. Siddharth had only one thing in his mind now, that should he ask her about the murderer. If she remembered him, then they would have to open the case again. He had left that house and he did not feel like going back.

After a few minutes, Siddharth went to the kitchen and prepared some quick noodles and coffee. After eating, they left for the hotel where they were staying and promised to return the next morning for Brinda. He pitied this small girl with so much load on her head.

Brinda was back for him… their love was pure…. she had left the world without saying goodbye…. maybe Brinda was reborn for him…...to speak the reality…. but the truth was still unknown…. he could feel that same fragrance again…. he could feel her presence…. it was not fake…but sordid realities had to be brought to the world again…to get the culprit hanged.

Siddharth couldn't sleep the whole night but lay on the balcony watching the stars confused, broken with memories of his love. The love that he had lost had now returned with grim realities. He had to make up his mind by morning.

He woke up late with the doorbell ringing continuously. His maid was standing at the door holding a basket of vegetables.

"Babuji…. what will you have for breakfast….and then what should I pack for lunch?" asked the middle-height Bengali maid wearing a yellow saree

"Prepare some aloo sabji (potatoes) with parathas for breakfast…. and we have three guests for lunch…. you can cook dal, rice and some vegetable."

Mr and Mrs Sarkar returned with Brinda by eleven. She looked pretty and now Siddharth noticed that her eyes were of the same grey colour as his wife. A reflection perhaps or a rebirth - everything was still lying covered like the moon under the clouds.

They discussed many other incidents of his life which she remembered. They decided to leave for Delhi the next day and reached early the next morning. After seven years, he was on the same road to house number 23.

He climbed the stairs slowly looking at the same walls that spoke of death and love. He reached the door; tiny Brinda came forward and took the keys. She remembered the right key and opened the door. The house was in a miserable condition with furniture covered with white bedsheets and dust and cobwebs everywhere. The kitchen was the same with her sarees still hanging in the cupboards. He switched on the lights and opened the windows.

The only thing troubling his mind was to ask the name of the murderer. She was a small child with her whole life in front of her and he didn't want to risk it for the second time. They cleaned the house and suddenly there was a knock at the door. Brinda ran to open it and a tall man was standing with a newspaper in one hand. He said, "I think we haven't met…. anyhow…I am Ashok. I live next door. If you need anything, you can call me…. I am the son of the old lady…she remembers you every day…. did you catch hold of the murderer…? She was such a gentle lady…...very sad."

Brinda had moved away on seeing him and peeped through the bedroom door. As he left Mrs Sarkar brought her to the drawing-room but she straight away ran to Siddharth breathing heavily and said, "He is the one…. he killed me." After saying this she fainted and they sprinkled water on her face. He shouted in anger, "You…. murderer…. I will kill you."

"Don't panic. We can call the police."

Brinda spoke in her childish voice, "He was repeating these words…. that old lady has started liking you…. you take care of her…. she praises you… has planned to hand over her house to you…. where will I go…. you deserve to be killed…I could smell alcohol and cigarette from him…. he was heavily drunk…. maybe he is the same till now."

Siddharth couldn't wait for a second now, as the culprit was right in front of him moving around freely. He knew he would have to explain to the police this rare case. He dialled the local police station and they reached in fifteen minutes. He explained the case and Brinda spoke dauntlessly explaining that evening's happenings. The police reached with them to the house next door.

Mrs. Sinha was surprised to see Siddharth with the police, "My son…you have come…….you are still searching for her murderer…. Almost eight years…see how she died…. I miss her every single day… my dear Brinda…. I loved her…. now I am sick, diseased….no one to take care…my son is here now."

"Where is your son…. aunty?" Siddharth asked, sitting next to her on the sofa.

"He is taking bath…I'll call him…. Ashok…. Ashok…. he has improved a lot…sometimes he gets angry…. rest he is fine…. Ashok," she kept calling his name and he came after five minutes. He was shocked to see police officials in front of him.

"What happened, ma?"

"I believe the investigation of Brinda murder case has begun again.... but if we knew.... we would have helped them."

The police officials came and caught Ashok who was about to run.

"Why? .... Why my son? .... Siddharth.... leave him."

"Madam, we will show you the clear picture of the murder.... your son is a murderer. He has been hiding for seven and a half years.... living a carefree life.... some secrets are disclosed.... when the right time comes," said one of the police officers.

Siddharth sat next to Mrs. Sinha and explained to her the unbelievable statements of Brinda. She was reborn to tell the naked truth of her murder. Mrs. Sinha was crying. She looked towards Ashok angrily and said in a loud voice with tears in her eyes, "Justice is done today…...Brinda…. you are back again…...how could I live with a scoundrel…cheater…. murderer?" She called young Brinda and hugged her tightly.

Ashok had no other way out so he accepted his crime and the punishment followed. Siddharth was at ease as the murderer was given life imprisonment for the serious offence. Mrs. Sinha decided to live with him in house number 23 with fond memories of Brinda. The young Brinda was relaxed and she loved to talk to Siddharth about all the incidents which she remembered.

After a few days, one morning Mr and Mrs Sarkar got ready with their luggage to leave for their hometown. Brinda looked alluring in a white frock and open hair. Siddharth had got used to talking to them but they had a life of their own. He couldn't live with them and they had to go on their separate ways. They had come from nowhere to help him out in solving the mystery of a lifetime. She too will grow up and live a life of her own. His Brinda had left for another world from where nobody returns.

"I am speechless…. I have no words of thanks. We will keep in touch…take care of Brinda and in future, if ever you need any help, I am always there…. we have a lifelong relationship now," said Siddharth and he moved forward to touch their feet.

Brinda came forward, held his hand and said with a smile as well as tears in her eyes, "Sid…. I am young…. I still have to see and experience this world…you loved Brinda…I am a part of her…she lives in me…but I ask you for one precious thing…. please."

"Yes…yes what can I do for you….? You are free to ask."

"You will have to wait for twelve years…. for me…. I will live with you…...spend my life with you…. marry you…. Please," Brinda said looking up to him and then to her parents. They couldn't say a word.

"I will…if you want and your parents agree…if destiny wants us to be together again…In this birth and the ones to come, I am yours…... Brinda."

# *Pandemic Love*

Shamim looked for an auto at the railway station but it was midnight and nothing was visible in the dim light at the railway station of Bareilly. Very few passengers had disembarked, as the country was facing a complete lockdown due to the pandemic. He walked on the road slowly for five minutes, keeping in mind the stray dogs who were busy following him -some barking, some wagging their tails on seeing him. Not a single soul was visible and the humid weather of April was already making him sweat.

Suddenly he saw an e-rickshaw and he waved at it shouting, "O rickshaw-wala…. please stop…. take me to Sunder Nagar…. …. how much money?"

The rickshaw stopped in the middle of the road and the driver, an old man with curly white hair and moustaches seeming more like a ghost, said in a thin voice,

"Sahib I will take two hundred rupees…. if you want you can sit…. it's up to you."

"You are charging too much…..…anyhow…. keep my luggage."

Shamim made himself comfortable in the rickshaw and they moved further on the ghastly road. They had reached midway when he saw two girls waving at the rickshaw.

"Who could they be at this time of the night?" he thought and told the rickshaw-driver not to stop. As they reached near, he rode the rickshaw fast but Shamim caught a glimpse of the girls and one of the faces seemed a bit familiar.

"Stop…. stop…. hey," he shouted and the man stopped it in the middle of the road. The two girls ran towards it and started pleading.

"Please help us…. please…. we are standing here for an hour."

Shamim told the rickshaw puller to stop so that he could lend a helping hand to these strangers. As the rickshaw drew closer, he tried to be alert as he had heard incidents of women thieves. He tried to recognize in the dim light the face and spoke excitedly,

"If I am not mistaken, you are Rehana…. we studied till class ten together in the Central School."

"Yes…. yes…you are Shamim…. I guess… it's been ages…. we can talk in the rickshaw."

How could it be possible…. the girl standing in front of him was the same whom he admired in school…the doe-eyed beauty with a twisted high ponytail…. all the boys of the class looked at her from the corner of their eyes but she preferred to stay aloof. He remembered her being obsessed with science subjects and being a favourite of teachers.

Shamim adjusted the luggage and they sat in front of them with one bag in his lap. The two girls had to get down on the way after one and a half kilometres.

He couldn't keep silent; he had so many questions in his mind so he began the conversation, "I think you too are returning home due to the lockdown. Where are you working?"

"We are returning from Lucknow…pursuing MBBS from the Government Medical College… we waited at the station for some time…there is nobody at home except my mother…. she couldn't come."

"Your father?"

"He is no more…he died last year of a heart attack," Rehana spoke in a sombre tone.

"Very sorry to hear that…may God give you strength."

They didn't talk much but his heart was beating faster than usual. Within fifteen minutes, they reached a small lane in Krishna Nagar. Rehana had introduced him to her friend Razia. It was pitch dark as she got down from the rickshaw and knocked on the door. Her mother switched on the light and opened the door. A middle-aged woman with streaks of grey hair covering her face with a dupatta, came out stretching both her hands as if to embrace.

"Come my child…Razia…how are you two…. I don't know what will happen to this world…. Allah knows better….in my whole life, I never heard about this disease…. Corona. She looked at Shamim and enquired, "Who is he?"

"Ammi… O Ammi…. Allah has sent us safely…he is my classmate…. Shamim…I don't think you remember him…. he made us sit in the rickshaw and agreed to drop us…. I am so thankful."

Rehana started picking up her luggage as the rickshaw puller was in a hurry.

"Be quick sahib…you made them sit …now you pay me hundred rupees more…come and sit fast."

Shamim sat inside and waved goodbye. He didn't want them to pay the money. He reached his home in another fifteen minutes and was welcomed by his parents and younger sister. Their servant Aladdin took the luggage to his room. After having dinner, he went to his room. Rehana kept disturbing him in his sleep as he had never thought that he would ever meet her again in this life.

Shamim awoke to a morning full of terror as his mother stood by him calling out his name loudly holding a glass of tea, "Wake up Shamim…. wake up…see what is happening in the world…did we ever think that we will have to see such days?"

She shook him and he started rubbing his eyes, "Ammi…it is only nine o'clock…my online work will begin at four in the evening…I don't know for how many months this will continue."

"Get up…empty your bags…. let me get all your suitcases, bags and clothes washed and sanitized."

Shamim had his tea and suddenly his eyes caught the attention of a strange black suitcase. It was quite similar to his own but it did not belong to him. He stood up and almost leapt towards it. He started examining it from all sides and caught hold of his head. On having a closer look, he saw Rehana scribbled with a red pen in one corner. The curfew in the city didn't even allow him to think any further. He simply picked the bag up and dumped it in his cupboard. He didn't want anyone else to see it. He emptied his bags and suitcase and locked his cupboard.

One evening when he entered his room he felt like vomiting. A foul smell seemed to be engulfing the room and he started checking all the objects. Suddenly he opened the cupboard and he smelled the suitcase lying in it. A strange pungent smell was coming from it. He took it out and kept it on the table. He had to open it as he knew no one would turn up till the situation returned to normal.

Shamim bolted his door and tried to open the bag but it was locked. He broke the lock and the suitcase threw open. Shamim almost fainted as he saw its contents. It was full of letters written in blood… probably fresh blood…. few medicines, syringes and injections. The entire room was filled with a musty smell. He covered his nose with his handkerchief.

"What the hell is all this?" he thought standing half bent. "Do students of MBBS carry such items with them?" His hands started trembling and he started fumbling with the letters. He knew it was sinful to read somebody else's letters, but Allah will forgive him. Everything happens for a reason.

He took the sanitiser lying on the table and sprayed it on the suitcase and other items. He wore his gloves and started collecting the items spread in the room. He opened one of the letters written with blood, and started reading it.

My Sweetheart,

Sarfaraz

Loving you is the best thing that happened …. but you ditched me…. for her…she is more beautiful…. I write every day….one letter …. with my red blood….one day only a drop will be left…. I will die.

Love you

Rehana

He could feel drops of sweat dripping from behind his ears. His curiosity grew and he picked up the second one.

My love,

You don't even look at me now…. remember the day we first met…you looked handsome in black…. I will keep on loving you…. will wait for you.

Rehana

Shamim brought the suitcase and arranged all the things scattered on the floor. There were more than fifty letters. He could make out that Rehana had been ditched in love. From the injections and pills, he could make out that maybe she had started taking drugs. Innumerable questions were arising in his mind and he closed the suitcase and kept it on the table. He would have to send it anyhow because it was not safe to keep these things at home.

There was no connection and he couldn't even go due to the lockdown. His whole day passed in uneasiness. He sat down to continue with his office work that night after dinner, when there was a sudden knock at the door. He got up to open the door and he was surprised to see a worried-looking man with short hair, probably in his thirties, standing at the door.

"Yes Sir. How can I help you?" Shamim asked from a certain distance.

"Are you Shamim….?  I am Feroze …...Rehana's brother."

"What can I do for you? I suppose you have come for…."

Suddenly he thought that maybe Rehana had not told them about the matters going on in her life. He preferred to remain quiet and listen.

"I have been searching your house for an hour…. that night you mistakenly brought her suitcase…I have come to take it…I need your help…. she hasn't been eating her medicines since that day…Rehana is unwell…admitted to the hospital."

"What? What happened? Which hospital?"

"Shivraj Hospital…it's nearby…we didn't get any bed in the Government hospital due to increasing number of Covid patients… She has sent me…... I think you have carried her suitcase by mistake."

"Yes …. yes …due to this lockdown I thought that I would go to return it once this comes to an end. You can take it…. but can I talk to her…? Is she in the condition to talk?"

"I'll call and see if she's awake or not."

They kept standing at the door for some time. Shamim took Feroze to the garden and offered him a chair.

"Come Shamim, she wants to talk to you," he called out and Shamim caught hold of the mobile, "Yes Rehana…. hope you are well."

She spoke in a low voice, "Shamim…...is it you…? My brother has come to collect my luggage…. I want to meet you…. can you please take out those letters and injections…….....please…? Then hand him the suitcase…....leave the tablets…....now this is no more a secret…. you can come once there are relaxations."

His heart melted for her the moment he heard her sobbing, "I'll do the required …. don't worry."

Shamim handed the mobile and went inside to bring her suitcase. He returned after five minutes and in the meantime, his parents had come to talk to this stranger. He handed the suitcase to Feroze and explained it to his parents.

A week passed and Shamim realised he had forgotten to take Rehana's phone number. It was a Sunday and there was a relaxation of five hours in the lockdown. The virus was spreading and with great difficulty, he got permission from his parents to go out for some time. Rehana had occupied his mind. He covered himself well, picked up the small bag in which he had carefully kept her things and went straight to the hospital.

At the reception, he told her name to the nurse and she replied, "Sir, her condition is critical…. she is in ICU…her family members must be there…. you go to the first floor." Shamim's hands started trembling; he placed the bag on the bench and sat down. He got up and moved towards the stairs. He recognized her mother and went up to her, "Aunty…. how is Rehana now…. that night she looked hale and hearty."

She started crying, "Oh…I don't know what happened to her… my Rehana……Oh Rehana… Allah save her."

He consoled her and asked her, "Can I meet her…....please?"

"Yes…go."

Shamim wore the kit that covered his head, mouth, and hands. He opened the door and saw that there were hardly two patients in the ICU. Rehana was lying unconscious on the bed surrounded by glucose bottles and oxygen cylinders. She shouldn't have been so serious in this relationship. Some boys take all this lightly but the innocent girls suffer. He moved forward and sat on the chair near her bed. He gathered courage and called out her name, "Rehana…. Rehana."

She didn't move. Then, he softly caught hold of her palm and called out, "Rehana…. can you hear me?"

She started opening her eyes and smiled at him.

"Sha..mim…..uh…when did you come…..my letters…..inject…tions…..you have….brought," she tightly held his hand and took it up to her face.

Tears started flowing and her pillow became wet.

"Shamim…. he married that girl…. he betrayed….me… Allah will punish him," she didn't know why was she discussing her love life with him. He was sitting in front of the girl whom he once secretly admired but times had changed, circumstances had changed and their positions differed.

"Don't feel bad…. you have your whole life lying in front of you…. you are in such a noble profession…. you are born to serve others…... live for others…don't spoil your life…... I remember the same young enthusiastic school girl…. who loved her subject Biology… ran around and had a gala time with friends…. you have to come back to life…. start your journey again," said Shamim with eyes moist.

"Can you come every day? …to guide me…motivate me…. maybe I will start living one more life again…. I feel rejuvenated…. please Shamim…my Ammi and Feroze know nothing."

"It is not possible except on weekends…. I'll try…. take care."

Shamim could sense some improvement in her while conversing. He asked her, "Although I should not interfere in your personal life but were you seriously taking drugs? You have to come out of it…the doctors must be treating you accordingly."

"Yes, I told them not to tell my family members."

Shamim started paying frequent visits and Rehana got discharged in a fortnight. He would sit for hours on weekends and they didn't realise the secret adoration that was growing between them. He made her laugh as well as cry. It was no more an infatuation but she couldn't forget her first love. The feelings of love for her were still hidden in Shamim's heart. He could not open up. Her mother too had started liking him.

She often said, "It is due to you that my daughter has come back.... school friends are a must...they are true friends."

Seven months passed and the situations improved. Shamim rarely visited Rehana's house as the conversations on the mobile phone increased. They were more of friends and would talk for hours. One day she called him up to tell him that she would be leaving for her college as she had to go for her internship.

It was a cold December morning when he reached her place to bid goodbye. He was to continue with his online work from home for two more months. The moment he entered her house wearing a black overcoat and muffler he looked quite stunning and Rehana looked up with a sad smile. She was leaving for Lucknow and the luggage was kept near the main door.

In these months she had shared the darkest secrets of her life with him and he  had never left her disheartened. She was sitting so convinced and hopeful because of him. He had been her guiding light in these months. Shamim had come for the final farewell with a hope that may be a spark is there in her.

He wished her mother and brother, "Salam Alaikum"

"Wa-Alaikum-as-salam...Come to my child.......we were waiting for you.... Shamim your presence gave her strength.... if you don't mind…Can I ask you one question?"

"Sure …sure," he answered with a faint smile.

She spoke to him with Rehana sitting next to her, "Can you take my daughter's hand in marriage…...? She has recovered now…hope she stays well…Rehana has grown fond of you in these months…... I have noticed her…...she feels so relaxed after talking to you…. she will never go against my decision…. she has full faith in me…. but her profession is different…she is very adjusting…I don't know about you…. but you can decide…I am not compelling you."

Shamim was on cloud nine as her mother was so understanding and he will marry the girl of his dreams. He was ready to accept her with all her faults. He knew deep down in his heart that it may take years for her to love him. He was ready, as destiny had brought them together. He knew very well that his parents would never refuse.

He said, "Aunty what you have thought is the best…I will say yes to this relationship. You can give it the name of Nikah…. you can come to talk to my parents."

Rehana gave him a pleasant smile with her eyes loaded with tears. She looked more heavenly in her green salwar-kameez.

She blushed and held her mother's hands, "Oh Ammi…. you care for me …. you want to see me settled…. I know you will do the best for me…love you…it's time to leave now…. I have to go to the station…. come on"

Shamim and Rehana sat together in the taxi and on the way, he said, "I hope you are ready to accept me as your shauhar…. I know it will be a bit difficult on your part…. but still"

"Of course…. Shamim…. we couldn't open up to that extent…... but parents know better about their children….one year is sufficient…. for love to grow…...we can name it Pandemic Love."

Both walked hand in hand on the platform and he waved her goodbye as the train moved further.

❖ ❖ ❖

# Arranged to Love

The cluttering of crockery and cutlery woke me up early on 7th February 1991. I had come to my Aunt's house in Kanpur from Jhansi to have a look at the boy which they had selected through my cousin's phone call. The families were known to each other but I had never seen him before. I was twenty-one, simple, elegant and unknown to the meaning of love. Five of them arrived in the evening - the boy, his father, sister, sister-in-law and an aunt. I wore a white salwar suit and in that same traditional manner was sent to sit with them so that they could have a look. "When will these customs change?" I thought…. so embarrassing if one refuses…. you are sitting like a zombie and the onlookers staring at you.

Hardly anyone can have a proper look as the situation becomes more gruesome when there is a call for the interview. You can never judge a person in a few hours as the secrets will be presented as a bunch of roses with an equal number of thorns once you become life partners. There were hardly any questions as his father looked like a saintly figure and the others remained in a silent mode, maybe scrutinizing the facts. The boy Vikram was not interested in conversation of any kind as he explained that he believes in destiny and respects his father's decision. My relatives were on cloud nine and started praising the guy before this relationship came into existence. I found him quite handsome but I thought that maybe the difference in complexion may bring a negative answer as our Indian community is still living with this outdated dialogue, "Gori bahu chahiye." (Need a fair-complexioned daughter-in-law)

After reaching home they gave their approval and my parents were super excited. Wishes started pouring in and the engagement was fixed for the fourteenth of April 1991. Preparations went on for two months with my parent's frequent visits to Kanpur. The red-letter day came when we exchanged rings. I was gifted a beautiful lotus ring and I wear it till today. I never wore any ring earlier because this was the one, I was waiting for. The marriage was fixed on the nineteenth of January 1992.

Having studied in a convent and being a voracious reader, the Mills and Boons hero was riding on a white horse in front of me. We had no mobile phones so I could only go to a Public Calling Booth and dial his number with cold hands.  Most of the times he was unavailable and I got an obnoxious reply from the other side, "You should wait till marriage. Ours is a very conservative family." My mind got so puzzled on hearing such strange comments but what mattered more to me was the choice and thoughts of the man I had to spend my life with. I kept sending letters and cards full of love through my mother.

Months passed and we met only once at my aunt's house. I could make out that he was a much responsible and mature person than I had thought him to be.  On the cold, foggy morning of the sixteenth of January 1992, I visited every room of my house with tears pouring down like a stream of the river. I went and sat down in front of my grandparent's photograph and my Waheguru. I said a silent prayer that this house prospers in my absence as I was always my dad's lucky charm. I reached Kanpur with my dad and my best friend since school days, Renu in the afternoon. My mother was already there doing the necessary arrangements.

On the morning of the nineteenth, I reached the venue accompanied by my beautician Lily. She caked and dressed me up in my exclusively embroidered heavy red salwar kameez with dupatta. At twelve we heard the sound of loud music with a singer singing in his monotonous voice, "*Aaj mere yaar ki shaadi hai* (My friend is getting married today) when my friend told me, "Mini, you should see the baraat…it is auspicious." I got up carrying a load of probably ten kilograms and went up to the window. The groom was sitting on the horse in a white coat pant and his face covered with the Sehra. To our surprise, he drew the golden strings of the Sehra and dumped them on his red turban. We could see someone handing over to him a rifle and he held it in such an expert manner as if he had practiced it. He efficiently caught the rifle facing towards the sky. He pulled the trigger and fired. My friend caught hold of my hand and said, "My God…Mini…. he is a real hero." I was left expressionless.

In the evening I was given a warm welcome by the family members. I was now his legally wedded wife. The space of a mother-in-law always remained empty. The rituals went on and my elder sister-in-law brought a tiny box filled with vermilion. I sat on the chair of my dressing table and my husband picked a pinch of it and filled my parting. That moment is still the most precious one and whenever I feel low, I go back to those unforgettable moments.

Living, knowing, judging and finally loving each other are the differences lying in an arranged and love marriage. I was witnessing these four stages and somewhat enjoying my life. He was my hero of this life. After a few days, we went for our honeymoon to Mussoorie. It was a pleasant trip as we visited many Gurudwaras and I liked the fact that he was equally religious.

My father-in-law was a gem of a person. He wanted me to continue with my studies. I joined the local college in my area and continued with my graduation. I got immense support from my husband as he knew the true meaning of literacy. I pitied him the day he came up to me after a few days of marriage and said holding my hand, "My mother died when I was in class nine and I couldn't pay attention to my studies…. losing a mother was the worst thing that happened in my life…. I want you to study and make our children literate….so that they can prove themselves…...live with their heads held high…...love you."

I was overwhelmed at the mere thought of continuing with my studies. The same year in November I gave birth to a beautiful daughter Vishakha. Days started flying and three things were on priority now

- daughter, husband and studies. Although he came on the second position now. In 1994, I gave birth to a healthy son Anmol and now my husband came in the third position.

Becoming a mother is the most adorable thing that happens after marriage. Love for my husband got somewhere hidden and we started enjoying the journey of bringing up our children in the best possible way. From the very beginning, I took a very strict decision of always sharing the daily issues, the good and the bad with my hubby. At times when I failed to explain something to my children, he did it better. Perhaps that was the love and bonding, between us and our children.

He always stood by and supported me in my literary journey. Earlier he had a misconception that if women start working in Punjabi families, the society will make fun of them. Slowly his thoughts matured with the growing years. Love can transform a person and I felt I had been successful in these years. When I stepped into the field of education I never looked back. After my post-graduation in 1999, I got admission in Doctorate. In 2002, I walked with him hand in hand with my degree. I could sense mixed feelings of joy and contentment on his face. The same year, I joined as a lecturer in a college and he was the happiest person on earth that day.

We live in a male-dominated society and I felt a matter of pride in walking with a man who was far more superior to me in all matters. He believed in the fact that his destiny changed the day I entered his life. My love for him never stagnated. If ever we had misunderstandings between us or children, I always went up to him and ironed out the differences. I believe in living peacefully and adjusting in all circumstances. Comparatively, I was calmer and more patient. I knew the more I hated him at times the more love poured from my heart.

Time flew. In October 2013, my daughter got married and my son cleared his Intermediate. On the eighth of November 2013, my son flew to London for further studies and my daughter to Dubai for her honeymoon. That day I couldn't stop my tears from flowing. After so many years we were standing at the airport alone, depressed, as I didn't know how to live without them. I had shared every bit of my life either happy or sad with my children but they have to live their own life.

I returned with my husband and love blossomed again. He started taking care of me; I felt rejuvenated. We started spending more time with each other and the same year, I joined as a school principal with increased responsibilities. Since then, life has taken many twists and turns and we have grown and faced the storms together. He knows the reason for my happiness and sadness. I can share the darkest secrets of my life with him and he listens to them patiently. He has a solution to every little problem of mine.

Who says arranged marriages don't lead to love? They do and it is a kind of love that is difficult to define. All marriages are based on compromises as no two people born in this world are similar. You get to know each other at a slow pace and the success ratio depends on both the partners. We have to learn the art of adjustment and a day comes when you become habitual of each other. Your morning begins with his smile and your day ends with a sweet 'Good Night'. I feel that my heart will go on and on for him and it happens with all those who love deeply.

*The End*